IT IS
Well

LETA BUHRMANN

To my husband and daughters.
Through each of you, I have witnessed God's amazing love.

PREFACE

I STILL REMEMBER THE MOMENT when I realized I was the woman at the well. Just like the biblical Samaritan woman whom Jesus met in John 4, I had suffered from guilt and shame for years. I was ashamed of my past—both the parts that weren't my fault and the parts that were. Fear that people would discover my many sins was my constant companion. I was always looking over my shoulder, worried that someone who knew the ugly truth would somehow destroy the new life I had tried to build. I felt unlovable. I built a wall around my heart, attempting to protect myself. Each broken relationship I had further reinforced my belief that I was unworthy of love and that I could only trust myself.

This novel is the story of one woman's journey as she reconciles with her own past and discovers that God's love is for everyone: even a broken woman. It is the story of a journey from brokenness to healing, love, and redemption, found in God's embrace. Just as Jesus met the Samaritan woman at the well, He will meet each of us. Even me. Even you.

Chapter 1

THE ROAD TO MY GRANDMOTHER'S FARM passed through the middle of Boresburg. I smiled at the name and wondered: do the teens in this small town still call it Boresburg? The state highway that eventually would lead me to my grandmother's home cut directly through this community of 3,500 people. I pulled up to one of the few stop lights in town and adjusted the mirror so I could see myself in it. I rarely studied my reflection. I was afraid I would be able to see directly into my soul, and that possibility was too scary for me. A quick glance reminded me that I no longer looked like the young girl who had moved away from here many years ago, so why did I always feel like that same sad, tormented child anytime I visited? There was something about this place, my hometown, that filled me with dread every time I returned. In my life away from here, I was more successful at covering my deep wounds. But on the farm, those wounds were exposed once again. They demanded to be seen, and there was no hiding from them.

When the light turned green, I readjusted my mirror and continued driving toward my past. How many years had I lived away? I'd been home for a few holidays since then, but those were only brief visits. And even those had dwindled recently. I had moved away immediately after high school . . . sixteen years ago. Was that possible? Had it really been that long? Feelings of anxiety and shame crept in, causing my heart to race, but I stuffed my emotions down with deep breaths. I stopped all my thoughts and memories and shut off the tears before they could even form. There was no time for that now anyway. I had been summoned home, and so home was where I had to go.

When I reached the edge of town, I felt compelled to turn onto Church Street. Grandmother told me when I was a child that the street had been named because the church was already there, built long before the roads had formal names. I spied the white, traditional clapboard-siding church, topped with a steeple and a bell, and pulled into a parking spot in front of the building, gripping the steering wheel tightly with both hands. How could a place hold such strong, mixed emotions and memories? My family had worshipped here for generations. This congregation had surrounded my grandparents and me through some difficult times. And, oh, how I'd loved to stand by my grandmother and sing harmony with her when I was a child.

There were certainly good memories here, but this was also the place where I'd heard stories that, for complicated reasons, I felt confident God's love wasn't meant for me. My sins were simply too great, and I convinced myself that God's love was only for others. This whiplash of emotions led me to avoid church after I moved away.

I sat, just staring at the church for several minutes as this flood of memories washed over me. I finally took several deep breaths, brought myself back to the present, and pulled back onto the state highway to continue my journey. Just a few minutes outside of town, I reached the country road that led to my grandmother's farm—the home where I had spent most of my childhood. Thankfully, the road was finally paved. For years, it had been just a dirt road. In the spring, when the rains wouldn't stop, it turned into a mud road. Grandmother's car could barely slug through it. Every time we tried, I thought we would end up stuck there in mud up to the bumper. Somehow, Grandmother knew exactly how fast to drive to avoid getting stuck.

Although the road was paved now, it was still wide enough for only one vehicle. I hoped I didn't meet someone coming toward me, because I wasn't sure whether my little sport car would make it with one set of wheels in the ditch. At this time of year, the ditch could be deceptively muddy from the recent winter thaw and the early spring rains.

I couldn't see it from this road, but I knew *his* house was only a few miles from where I was. The anxiety I felt at the memory and the proximity of his house made it difficult for me to drive. Simply thinking about him caused me to experience a panic attack, and I fought to keep my breathing even. I had to summon all my strength to keep moving forward. I thought of him only as *the boy* because I didn't want to acknowledge anything about him—not even his name. Such pain could be buried only so deep, and it was now rushing to the surface. The thought of seeing him was more than I could handle, and I fervently hoped he had not moved back here.

I came up over a slight rise in the road and could finally see my grandparents' house off to the left, up a gravel drive. In my mind, the two-story white house seemed to dwarf the countryside, and had stood there since time began. It was certainly at least a hundred years old. Generations of my family had lived there over the years. An unusual lump found its way in my throat at that thought.

The farm was a striking sight. Grandmother had always loved

3

having a white house and a red barn. The barn was farther back from the road, but it was clearly visible on this flat farm ground. I was thrilled when I saw the apple orchard was still standing. As a girl, I'd loved to spend time there. Even though it was not far from the house, I had always felt that I was entering a different world when I walked into the orchard. I would often climb the trees. When I was a teenager, I would take a book and spend hours reading in their shade. The breeze was so refreshing on a hot day. Of course, there was always so much to do on the farm that I didn't get to sit and loaf every day. Many days were spent working in the hot sun, but in those glorious moments when there was time to relax, I always went to the orchard.

Most of the work I did was helping my grandmother harvest our enormous garden and then can and freeze the bounty. Grandmother had refused to purchase fruits and vegetables. She believed home-grown food tasted better and was better for you. It was backbreaking work at times, but over time, I realized that nothing purchased in a store could come close to the taste of what we raised. Grandmother had been right—the hard work had been worth it.

I reached the familiar gravel driveway and followed its slight curve all the way up to the house. It looked exactly as it had for many years. The buds on the trees were swollen, and their leaves were preparing to open. The early spring flowers were just poking through the dirt and would soon brighten the farm with their beauty, but I didn't truly notice any of this. Memories, thoughts, and emotions were swirling in my mind.

When I finally opened the car door, I immediately heard music pouring out of the open upstairs windows. Though there might be more cold days to come, the warmth of this day brought the welcomed promise of a warmer season approaching. Strains of the hymn "Will the Circle Be Unbroken" floated on the breeze down to where I stood. Grandmother preferred the original lyrics, and that was the version I heard.

There are loved ones in the glory
Whose dear forms you often miss,
When you close your earthly story
Will you join them in their bliss?

Will the circle be unbroken
By and by, yes, by and by?
In a better home awaiting
In the sky, in the sky.

You can picture happy gath'rings
'Round the fireside long ago,
And you think of tearful partings,
When they left you here below.

Will the circle be unbroken
By and by, yes, by and by?
In a better home awaiting
In the sky, in the sky.

One by one their seats were emptied,
One by one they went away,
Now the family is parted,
Will it be complete one day?

Will the circle be unbroken
By and by, yes, by and by?
In a better home awaiting
In the sky, in the sky.

The song put a small smile on my face. Gospel music had surrounded me as a child, but lately, I never took the time to enjoy music of any kind. I focused all my energy on my career, and there was no time left for leisure activities. Besides, gospel music was too painful. The message, the memories—it was all too much.

I turned my attention back to getting my suitcase from the car but was interrupted with the words, "One by one their seats were empty, one by one they went away." I stopped and looked up at my grandmother's bedroom window again. Could she really be ready to pass to the other side? The emotions of this thought caught in my throat. This was not the sort of reaction I was expecting. Of course this day would come for Grandmother; death comes for everyone. I was surprised by the sadness that was creeping in. I prided myself on always being the calm, cool professional. Emotions were left to others. After all, I had spent years perfecting how to control my emotions, and now, I was shocked that they were about to boil over onto the surface.

When my aunt, Lu, called to tell me that I needed to come home, I was at work and didn't want to process the significance of what that meant. She had called me at my office because she knew that was the only place to find me, and she'd told my secretary that it was a family emergency. Even though I was busy, I finally took the call.

"Aunt Lu, I'm in a meeting. I can't talk now," I had told her.

"Honey, I know you're busy," Aunt Lu had gently said, "but

it's your grandmother. The doctor doesn't think she will live much longer, and she wants to see you one last time."

"Look, thank you for letting me know. I promise I will call you later tonight, but I need to get back to this." I hung up the phone. Considering the serious nature of her words, it was probably rude of me to end it so abruptly.

Her call had bothered me all day. I couldn't focus. Even though I pretended I was fine and put forth a brave face for my colleagues, the thought of my grandmother nearing the end of her life bothered me in a way I couldn't explain. I simply didn't like to think about anything that pertained to my past—and, unfortunately, that included my family. So, this emotion I was feeling caught me off guard. I imagine some people would call me coldhearted, but the intense pain I felt from my past had caused me to wall off that part of my life. It was a bad coping mechanism, but it was the only one I knew. I called home later that evening, and my aunt repeated what the doctor had said: Grandmother didn't have much longer to live. There was nothing more that could be done for her.

Much to my own surprise, I decided that I needed to go home immediately. What surprised me the most was the urgent pull I felt to go. I made plans for my business partner and a few other key employees to cover my work. I told everyone that I didn't know when I would be back, but that I didn't think I would be gone for a prolonged period. I simply wanted to check on my grandmother and have a brief visit. Then I would return.

Chapter 2

DO I RING THE DOORBELL, *or do I just walk in?* I wondered. This had been my childhood home for years, yet I felt a bit like a stranger. Still, it seemed odd to ring the doorbell of a house that I had called home for so many years. *What a ridiculous debate,* I finally realized. I rang the bell. It didn't take long for someone to come to the door.

"Why, it's Lydia!" Aunt Lu exclaimed when she saw me. "Why are you ringing that doorbell? Come in here and have some coffee cake. I made it for tomorrow's breakfast, but I think you could use a piece now. You must be tired and hungry after your drive."

Aunt Lu was my widowed aunt. She and her husband, Vern, never had children. After Uncle Vern died, Lu moved into the farmhouse to help care for the farm—and eventually for her mother as well. Lu was just about the best cook in the world, and she was famous in the community for her baked goods.

As soon as I stepped inside the old house, I once again felt like I was a little girl. The smell of cinnamon coffee cake filled my nose, and I had to acknowledge that I had come home. I nearly fainted as I realized just how hungry I was. But before I could eat, I had to know.

"How is she?" I asked.

"It's her time, honey," Aunt Lu said. "I am just so glad you came home. She's been holding on to see you. I hope that wasn't too blunt, but it is the truth."

The lump in my throat was now so big that I had a difficult time swallowing. How could so many emotions run through a person all at once? I didn't know if I could handle this. It was simply too much to process—feeling like a child, but knowing I was an adult. I felt as if I were about to lose all composure. This was what I had feared. Suddenly I was the insecure, constantly in pain little girl again.

Just a few hours ago, I had been the in-command-of-myself-and-my-emotions lawyer and lobbyist. People were amazed at my ability to maintain composure under the greatest of pressures. And now, the aroma of a coffee cake and hearing the news that our family matriarch was waiting to die so she could see me—it was almost too much. I had to take a deep breath to regain my composure so that I could face anything I heard and handle any memory that might creep up on me.

"Would you like some coffee with your cake, dear?" Aunt Lu asked, breaking into my thoughts.

"Maybe in a little bit," I said. "Is Grandmother in her room?"

"The doctor is with her now. Why don't you have something to eat and then go visit?"

"I'd like to hear what the doctor has to say."

"Of course, honey. Go on up."

Aunt Lu seemed to know it would serve no purpose to argue. Even as a child, when I had a determined look in my eye, it was almost impossible to dissuade me. I guessed she also knew that I wanted to hear for myself exactly what the doctor had to say.

I climbed the familiar stairs to the farmhouse's second story.

The fourth step creaked just like it always had. Funny how such a strange thing like a creaky step could be comforting. It must represent some continuity. Even when so many things were changing, some things stayed the same. My room was to the right, and my grandparents' room was to the left.

I knocked gently on the door to Grandmother's room and heard her voice say, "Come on in, child."

I opened the door and stepped into Grandmother's bedroom. Walking into this room was always like stepping into the past. The bed, dresser, and rocking chair were in the exact same locations that I remembered. The wallpaper was the same busy floral pattern that Grandmother loved. She always said she loved sleeping in a Victorian flower garden. As a child, I would try to count all the flowers, but I always ended up with a headache from the eye strain. Everything was exactly as it had always been; the only thing that looked different was my grandmother. The years showed on her face. Her wrinkles were deeper, and her eyes were more sunken. Even her skin looked older. It had an almost translucent glow.

"How did you know it was me, Grandmother?"

"I heard a car pull in," she said. "You know those tires on the gravel always give away the surprise. Then when Dr. Woods said, 'That sure is a sporty red car,' I knew it had to be you."

Grandmother looked so old—older than I remembered—but of course, she was. She was ninety-six. How did that happen? How did the years sneak by so quickly? Why had I not come sooner? Regret upon regret came rushing in.

"Are you in any pain?" I asked.

"Just a little, child."

Child. It irritated me whenever Grandmother called me that.

She must have sensed my irritation, because she called me over to get a better look and took my hand. "My sweet child. Look at you." She smiled at me as she spoke to the doctor. "You know, Dr. Woods, Lydia isn't really a child anymore. She is an extremely successful lawyer and lobbyist in Washington, DC. Can't you just imagine her at work? With that determined look on her face, I suspect the others just say, 'Yes ma'am' to her."

I had to smile. It was the first time I had ever heard my grandmother acknowledge that I was an adult.

"I need to be going, Mrs. Roberts," said Dr. Woods. "I will stop by and see you again." He walked over to the bed and patted her hand. "In the meantime, I know you are in good care with Lu, and now Lydia's here too."

"Grandmother, I'm going to walk Dr. Woods out, if you don't mind. I'll be back in just a moment."

Grandmother had that devilish little grin that she would get when she knew what I was up to. "There's no need to be polite, child. I know you want to talk to the doctor about me. It's all right. You go talk to him. Then you come right back up here and talk to me. I just have to know what is going on in our nation's capital."

I nodded. There was no discussion with Grandmother; I *would* be right back to talk to her.

When we reached the first floor, I asked, "So, Dr. Woods, are you the last doctor in America who makes house calls?"

He chuckled. "Your grandmother is one of my oldest and most-delightful patients. I knew it would be a challenge to bring her to the office. It's the least I could do. Besides, that aunt of yours always feeds me when I come, so perhaps my intentions are also self-serving."

I hated this idle small talk. I wanted to get right to the point, so I did. "Well, how is she? Will she recover?"

"She is ninety-six years old. What do you think?"

"I suppose not." The depth of the sadness in my heart was difficult to process. I was, once again, on the verge of a breakdown because my ninety-six-year-old grandmother, with whom I had not spent any significant time in years, was on the verge of death. I needed to harden up a little more if I was going to get through this.

"What, uh . . . what is wrong, exactly?"

"It's her heart. She's had problems with it for years. Now, it's just wearing out."

"Isn't there some medication or something else that can be done?"

"She has been on medication for quite some time. Now, nature is just running its course."

"I see." The realization that my grandmother would soon die was beginning to sink in.

"Lydia," Dr. Woods said after a moment, "how are you doing? I don't intend to upset you, but you look exhausted. Are you taking care of yourself?"

"I'm fine," I said abruptly. He was right; I was irritated. He was no longer my doctor, and I felt that I was fully capable of managing my minimal health needs. "I'm just tired from the trip."

"If you need anything while you're here, just let me know. Feel free to stop by the office."

I assumed that he still remembered, from years ago, I'd had some health issues that were never resolved. I was always scared he would discover the true cause of my physical problems. Even though he wasn't a psychiatrist, he probably knew I was depressed during my teenage years. My real fear was that he would discover why. Even though I didn't like to think about it, there was also a time when I was hospitalized. During that stay, I overheard the doctor telling Grandmother that if ever there was a lost soul, I was one. I remember blinking back tears and thinking that was a perfect description of me.

"Yes, of course, I will." I managed a small smile and changed the subject. "Would you like something to eat?" That was my way of saying, *I'm fine, and that is the end of this conversation.*

He didn't seem to care for such a dismissal, but he ignored it. "I do believe I'll stop and visit with your aunt for a minute."

Chapter 3

I KNEW THAT IF I didn't immediately go back upstairs to visit with Grandmother, I would soon receive a summons. I knocked softly on the door, hoping Grandmother had nodded off to sleep. What could—or should—I say after hearing the doctor's prognosis? Facing death was not something I was good at, and I was dreading this journey with my grandmother.

"Come in and visit a while," Grandmother said rather weakly, dashing any hopes that she'd fallen asleep.

She looked even more tired than she had just a few minutes ago. This sight struck me. With honest compassion, I asked, "Should I come back later so that you can rest, Grandmother?"

"No, child, I'll rest in a moment. Sit right down here," she said, patting the edge of her bed. "I'm so glad you are here. I prayed that you would come. It is so nice to have you home.

"I'm going to just jump right into this. I'm going to speak to you with some honesty and bluntness. My time left here is short. I feel certain that Jesus will call me home soon, and there are some important things I need to say. I don't have the strength to share them all right now, but I need to tell you soon. There are some things you need to hear.

"I will apologize now if I offend you, but when you are at this point in life, you just have to say things. All I ask is that you reflect on them, because I feel they are ordained by God for me to say to you. You might not understand everything immediately, but I am confident that in time, you will."

I simply sat and listened. I hoped my face didn't reflect the deep fear I felt. What on earth could God want Grandmother to say to me? I had to summon every essence of stoicism I possessed to sit but not speak or flee the room.

"I have known for years that you are not happy. I know your life has not been easy, child, but most people do not have an easy life. Losing your parents was hard. It was hard on your grandfather and me too. A parent should not have to bury a child. Of course, I know it was more difficult for you. It is tragic to go through childhood and adolescence without your parents.

"I also know how difficult it was to come and live with us. We weren't young when your father was born, and he was a bit older when you were born, so I'm sure you felt that you had *old* grandparents. Again, I recognize that your life has not been easy, but you need to hear this. You must move on! Sometimes our lives are difficult and we face tragedies, but we must not stop and allow ourselves to wallow in sadness. We do not often understand why these things happen. They just do. Hopefully, we can learn some lessons from our struggles. At the very least, we need to know that we are not alone and that we will grow stronger from them. We must keep moving forward.

"I also know that something happened to you when you were a teenager. I had begun to see healing in you after your parents died, but then something changed and you went right back into the cave where you had lived. Now, child, I don't know *what* happened, and I guess after all these years, it doesn't matter what it was. What *is* important is that you realize this is what

I was telling you about. Something hard and horrible may have happened, but you must face it and then move on. If you want to talk to me about it, you are welcome to. If you want to find someone else to talk to, then you are welcome to do that too. But this cave you live in—you cannot go on living there. Some people would say that you're putting up a wall around yourself. Whatever you call it, it must be changed. Do you know why?"

For the first time in several minutes, I spoke. My voice was strained a bit, but I allowed no tears to fall. "No, Grandmother. Why must it be changed?"

She struggled to pull herself up in her bed. "Because you are not really living." The fire in her eyes was obvious. *This* was the grandmother I remembered from my youth. "You are not living. You are merely surviving. Is that what you want out of life— simply to survive it? Do you want to lay your head down at night and say, 'Well, I survived another day'? You didn't live it! You breathed. You ate. You went through the motions of a career, but you did not live."

I couldn't believe this lecture. This was coming from a woman who was about to die? I wondered how much longer she could go on. And what did she mean by "the motions of a career?" I could name any number of people who would love to have my career. But yet, there was a voice somewhere deep inside, asking if there might be at least some truth to what she was saying.

Grandmother took a deep breath and continued. "When was the last time you heard a cricket chirp or a bird sing? Or when was the last time you noticed a majestic tree or a beautiful flower? How about the last time you enjoyed music, a book, a play—anything? When was the last time you laughed so hard and so long that your stomach hurt? When was your last meaningful conversation with another person? And what about the last time you thanked God for the blessings He has given you?

"I know you must blame God for taking your parents and for all the other pains in your life, but He has also given you many blessings. He gave you grandparents and aunts and uncles who love you dearly. He gave you an amazing brain and a drive to succeed. He has blessed you with the ability to put clothes on your back and a roof over your head. When are you going to thank Him for those things?"

"I wouldn't even know what to say," I said quietly. My hands lay in my lap, and I focused my eyes on my shoes. The anger and guilt over my past, the sadness from Grandmother's prognosis, and so many other emotions that I could not even acknowledge swirled together and threatened to overwhelm me if I even glanced at her. I dared not look up at this moment.

"All God wants is the absolute best for you," Grandmother said, her voice gentle. "Are you living the best life you can live for Him?"

"What does that even mean?" I asked.

"I think you need to have a conversation with Him on this subject. God wants you to be happy. He does not want this constant gloom. He does not want this plastic face that refuses to show emotion. He wants a soul with life and passion in it! I know you are a serious-minded person, but there was once joy in that soul of yours. There was a time when you would get so excited about something that you could not contain yourself. Where is that part of you, Lydia?"

Grandmother seemed to be using all the energy she could muster for this lecture. It was obvious that she had waited a long time to have this talk with me.

"Your face—and I wonder if your heart too—has gone so long without emotion. Do you even know how to feel anything anymore?"

I felt myself withdraw a little more with every sentence, and I worked hard to suppress the anger I felt. For as long as I could remember, I'd had a river of anger flowing through me that I refused to acknowledge. Weren't emotions like anger and sadness for those who were weak? Wasn't happiness meant for people who were just going to be disappointed anyway? And wasn't showing emotion exposing your soul? That would mean being vulnerable, and I would not be vulnerable! Not anymore.

"What do you want from me, Grandmother? What do you want me to say or to do?" I spoke deliberately and slowly, doing my best to keep my feelings in check.

"I have already told you, child. I want what God wants for you. I want you to live the full life that He has ordained for you. I want you to live a life that is wide awake to all the beauty and majesty that He has created and given us—the best! That is what He wants, and that is what I want for you.

"You are a special person. You have been given many talents and gifts. How are you going to spend those? To whose glory will you use those gifts? When you go to bed at night, I want you to be able to say, 'This has been a fabulous day, and I lived every second of it. What a joy and honor it was! I greeted the morning and spent the whole day living—not surviving or simply bearing every single second, but truly living.'

"This life is a gift. There is no dress rehearsal. We have one chance to live! Go, child. Live. That is what I want. Remember, I told you that I wanted you to ponder what I had to say. You will need to think and pray about all of this. You will need to speak to God to see what you should do with it."

Grandmother paused for a moment and let her eyes close. She took a breath. "My energy has left me for now, but I will have more to share soon. I have so much that I've waited to say."

I didn't know how I could possibly handle any more of these talks. This one had already brought me to the edge. I had lived a measured existence for many years, and I refused to change that simply because I was home. I also needed time to process. What was that voice I heard asking if there was some truth in what Grandmother said? Was there something I needed to hear?

I stood and leaned over to kiss Grandmother's forehead. "Get some rest. I'll see you later."

As I walked down the stairs, my stomach growled a loud reminder that I hadn't taken Aunt Lu up on her offer of food. I knew I needed something to eat. I needed all my strength—physical, mental, and emotional—for this trip.

Chapter 4

AUNT LU WAS RIGHT WHERE I knew she would be—in the kitchen. She was a short, heavyset woman. Many people thought I looked like a thinner, younger version of her. There was a definite family resemblance. She "loved" everybody with food, and she was an excellent cook. Her pies were known throughout the entire county. Her husband, Uncle Vern, had died a few years earlier after a long battle with lung cancer. Smoking had finally caught up with him. When he started smoking, no one knew it was bad for your health, and he had told me over and over when I was young never to start the habit. He just couldn't stop, and by that time, the damage was already done.

Aunt Lu moved in with Grandmother after that, which was the only reason that Grandmother had been able to continue living in this house. Without assistance, it just would not have been possible. The house was too big, and her health issues were too great to handle the farm alone.

My aunt was taking off her apron as I walked in the kitchen. The room looked much the same as it had in my childhood. The oven had to be more than thirty years old, but since it worked, Grandmother kept it instead of upgrading to something more modern. There was no microwave, but why would they need one? They were never in a hurry to prepare a meal. Both Grandmother and Aunt Lu preferred recipes that simply couldn't be hurried. What I loved most about the kitchen was the antique table. It could fold down to take up less space, but there was never a time I could remember when it had been folded. It was always set up to feed at least six people. Grandmother said, "You just never know who might stop by needing something to eat."

"Are you hungry?" Aunt Lu asked. "You never ate anything when you arrived. You didn't even sit down for a minute before you rushed up to see your grandmother. I took some leftover pie crust and made an individual pie for you while you were upstairs. Would you like that? Or would you rather have that coffee cake I promised? Maybe you need them both!"

I was certain I would gain at least ten pounds on this trip. How could I decline the absolute best pie crust in the world? My mind flashed back to when I was a child, and I would help Grandmother bake pies. My favorite part was when she would say that there was a little too much pie crust left over. She would sprinkle cinnamon and sugar on the dough, roll it up, and bake it. Sometimes Grandmother would even take an apple and make a little pie out of the extra dough. It was like an apple turnover, but it was so much better because it was a whole pie I didn't have to share! Grandmother had always made little pies just for me. Not only were they amazingly delicious, but they made me feel so special. And now, Aunt Lu had made a pie "just for one." What wonderful memories!

"I would love a little pie," I confessed. "I didn't realize how hungry I was. When I'm done, how about I help you clean up? I can't have you cooking for me like this and not do something to help."

Aunt Lu smiled and kissed me on the cheek as she handed

me a plate. "I'm so glad that you're home. You will be good medicine."

At that comment, I wondered, *good medicine for whom*? If Grandmother was truly nearing the end of her life, would my presence help in some way?

I let go of that thought as I sat down at the table and took a bite of the pie. Warm apple and a hint of cinnamon filled my mouth, and my eyes rolled backward as I savored the first bite. I had never eaten pie anywhere else that came close to the wonderful taste of my family's recipe. It was divine.

Aunt Lu hovered over me while I ate. "How is it, dear? It's your grandmother's recipe, of course. I've never found a better one for pie crust."

"Fabulous. Simply fabulous," I mumbled between bites.

"I'll get started washing these dishes. You enjoy, and then you can help finish up if you'd like."

I thoroughly enjoyed every bite. I couldn't remember when I had eaten anything that tasted this good. Of course, I couldn't really remember the last genuinely good meal I had eaten. When the pie was gone and I had licked the fork clean, I got up to help my aunt.

There were always so many dishes to do. Grandmother never wanted a dishwasher. She said that hand-washing the dishes gave her time to look out the window and enjoy looking at God's creation—His beautiful handiwork with the flowers, the orchard, and the fields just beyond. Doing the dishes gave her time to reflect and thank God for all His blessings.

It was strange how these thoughts came back to me the longer I stood there. As we worked, we chatted about the weather and local news. Just catching up filled the entire time it took to handle that load of dishes.

As soon as the dishes were complete, Aunt Lu said it was time to begin working on dinner.

"We just finished cleaning up!" I said.

"Yes, I know," Aunt Lu said with a smile. "But that's the way farm work is. Do you remember?"

"I'm beginning to. Maybe all this work is why I left." I grinned.

"I think you probably work more hours at your job than we do on this little farm, dear. I can never reach you at home."

"I guess I do work a lot of hours, but they're not all spent standing on my feet."

"Yes, I suppose you're right. You must sit for most of your work. Think how big I would be if I sat around all day."

I found myself surprised that I felt so comfortable talking with my aunt. Of course, I hadn't visited with my family often since I became an adult. I had been quiet and introverted as a child, and the minute I became an adult, I moved away to go to college and hadn't returned. I wondered if life was different now and we somehow had more in common.

As night approached, I grew apprehensive knowing that I would eventually have to face my old room. I had not spent a pleasant night there in years. Whenever I closed my eyes to fall asleep, all those old memories and feelings would haunt me. I would either stay awake for hours, reliving horrible memories, or I would have nightmares all night long. But the trip to the farm and seeing my grandmother had exhausted me, and I knew I needed sleep.

Chapter 5

WHEN I HAD PUT OFF SLEEP as long as possible, I went to my old room. It was a beautiful bedroom and completely clean. The antique canopy bed looked as if I had slept in it the night before. The quilt my grandmother had made was still on the bed. My writing desk was still there too, and everything I had left on the dresser was in the same place where I'd left it. A picture of me as a young girl, smiling and sitting on my mother's lap with my father standing behind us, hung on the wall in the same spot it always had. I wondered why Grandmother had never moved anything— except to clean, of course.

The room had three huge windows that let in a great deal of natural light—one facing north, one west, and one east. I moved the desk chair to the north-facing window and sat down. How many hours had I spent sitting here, gazing out this window and thinking about what-ifs and what-shoulds? The reason I dreaded being in this room was because this was the only place where I allowed myself to think about and remember what had happened when I was young.

My breathing involuntarily increased in speed, and I took a deep breath and exhaled slowly. I told myself I would not hyperventilate; I was an adult, and my adolescent decisions and mistakes were behind me . . . weren't they? Deep in my soul, I knew my past still tormented me because I had never confronted it or my pain. Was it time to face those demons and do something about them? Was it time, finally, to move forward? But how does one put the past behind them and leave it there? Somehow, I wondered if I could.

Memories flooded my mind before I could stop them. There he was: the boy who had been so handsome in my eyes. He was tall, with dark hair, and even darker eyes. I was considered quite plain-looking by my peers. I didn't know how to style my hair or how to wear makeup like the other girls, and I honestly didn't care about such things anyway. My glasses, which were large and completely out of style, did nothing to enhance my appearance. My lack of fashion sense simply added to my awkwardness. The only thing most people noticed about me was that I was bright. Unfortunately, that wasn't considered important in the social order of my peers.

Then *he* came along, and I thought everything had changed.

For the first time in a long time, I felt loved. I couldn't explain why I didn't feel love before. I knew in my head that my family loved me, but for some reason, I never truly felt it in my heart. *He* wanted to be with me. *He* wanted to hug me and love me, and I enjoyed being with him.

The night of our date, he picked me up, and we went to a movie. The name of the movie was soon erased from my memory.

On the way home from the movie, he pulled into a deserted county park. The entrance gates were closed, but he jumped out to move them. I rolled down the window and questioned his actions. "Won't we get caught being in here when the park is closed?"

"Don't be silly," he said, a mischievous grin on his face. "Who would even know?"

"Why are we coming here, anyway?"

"There's a beautiful place where we can gaze at the stars. I want you to see it. It'll be fine," he said.

We drove through a heavily wooded area until there was a clearing with a few parking spaces. Off to the right was a boat launch leading into the lake. He pulled into a spot facing the water and turned off the car.

"It's so crowded up here," he said, flashing another smile and giving me a wink. "We'll have more room if we move to the back seat." Something told me that this was a bad idea, but I wanted to be close to him. I felt protected in his arms. We climbed into the back seat.

"I love you so much," he said when we were situated again.

I leaned my head on his shoulder and gave a contented sigh. "I love you too."

"I just want to hold you and kiss you." And he did. But the kisses soon became longer and more passionate. I could hardly breathe.

Then he began to unbutton my shirt.

"No," I told him.

"C'mon, sweetheart. You're so beautiful. I want to touch you."

I knew I should make him stop, but for some reason I couldn't. Soon, he unzipped my pants. I squirmed, trying to stop him.

"Just let me touch you," he said. "There is nothing wrong with that. We love each other, don't we?"

The terror I felt was so strong that I couldn't move or speak. I was paralyzed. Somewhere, deep down, I knew this was wrong.

I wanted him to stop, but I still thought I could trust him. Conflicting emotions warred within me.

He took off his clothes and guided my hand to touch him. I had never done anything like this, and the sheer panic inside me was unbearable. He climbed on top of me, but I was still too frightened to move or speak.

I finally heard a voice yell, "Stop. This is wrong! No!" I don't know if it was only my soul yelling or if I had been able to scream out loud, but he didn't listen.

"I love you. It's okay," he said over and over.

On the verge of hysteria, I cried, "No, it's wrong!" But it was too late.

I was so confused. My now raw emotions told me repeatedly that this was wrong. After it was over, he kissed me again.

"Wasn't it wonderful? I love you. I love you so much." He whispered it again and again. All I felt was guilt, fear, panic, and utter shame. No, there was absolutely nothing wonderful for me.

I felt numb. How had this happened? *What* had just happened?

It seemed that someone else was crying out with me. Was that God? Was it just me, alone? Without really understanding what it was, I knew that something in my inner core had been shattered. In one brief, unwanted moment, my entire world had been altered, and my innocence had been ripped away. My soul was devastated.

He kissed me again and held me, and he told me everything was fine. He acted like nothing wrong had happened. I sat there unable to move. Outwardly, I was without emotion. I was in shock. Although I had not wanted or planned this to happen, it *had*.

Immediately, I internalized that this was somehow my fault. *Girls who don't want this to happen don't get in the back seats of cars with boys,* I thought. *Girls who don't want this to happen don't allow someone to take their clothes off. Girls who don't want this to happen do everything they can to make their boyfriends stop.* I had been paralyzed to act, so I was sure that meant this was my fault. My head was spinning. A part of me felt that I was a victim. But at the same time, I also believed that this was my fault, and that meant I couldn't be a victim of anything but myself.

We stayed in the car for a while, looking at the night sky. He pointed out various constellations to me, but I didn't care about the stars. I simply sat, looking straight ahead. He finally drove me home, acting as if nothing unusual had happened. He kissed me good night, and I went inside the house. I told my grandmother good night, as was our routine when I had been out, and then I went straight to my room.

In my room, I thought I would feel safe. Nothing else could hurt me there, and Grandmother would not see me and become suspicious that something was wrong. As was my custom when I wanted to think, I pulled my desk chair to the window and sat down. But instead of providing comfort, my room seemed to close in around me. The walls appeared to be moving in to suffocate me. I quickly realized that it was my own out-of-control breathing, and I tried to relax. But when I couldn't, I grabbed my teddy bear and squeezed him with all my might. The tears that were building inside of me refused to come.

The next few days were a blur. I was not myself, but I did seem to be able to function at some level. I'm sure my grandmother noticed that I was quieter than normal and that I spent a lot of time sitting in the orchard. Since I was a teenager, perhaps she expected some moodiness; I don't know. At least she didn't say anything to me about it.

Monday finally came, and I was completely baffled by how the boy acted at school. He paraded around like something incredible had happened to him, strutting around everywhere. I wondered if he had said anything to anyone. My fears were confirmed when his buddies slapped him on the back and congratulated him right in front of me. One of his friends even told me, "When you get tired of that loser, feel free to call me." And then he smiled and gave me a knowing wink.

I was mortified by his comment and by the fact that my boyfriend hadn't said anything to defend me. I had no words to describe how completely ashamed and embarrassed I felt.

After everyone went to class, I pulled him aside. "Did you tell anyone what happened at the park?" I asked.

He looked at me as if I had lost my mind. "Of course I did. Why are you so upset? You had sex with me. Now you'll finally be popular!"

I immediately realized that would not be true. "You may be more popular because you had sex. I'm just an easy target of unwanted attention, and now every guy in school thinks I'll have sex with him. I wanted you to love me, and all you did was take advantage of me!" I yelled.

"I'm going to class," was his only response.

Chapter 6

HAVING THE PRECIOUS GIFT of my innocence taken away by someone who didn't care about me at all was devastating. He took something that wasn't his to take. He had simply wanted physical pleasure and the illusion of looking like a man in front of his friends. I, however, had been searching for love—a permanent and authentic love. It felt as if a part of me had been killed and what was left was slowly dying.

Even though I didn't completely understand, I knew that a part of my inner core had been tragically damaged. In essence, the values that were a part of my being had been broken. My core value of trusting loved ones had been ripped away in an instant. My self-respect and honor had been stolen. My idea of what true love looked like had vanished. Perhaps most significantly, my belief that God would protect me from harm was annihilated. I felt abandoned by God—and by myself as well. I had been dramatically changed without my permission.

Having my core values damaged in such a traumatic way was numbing. This incident caused me to separate myself from God because of my shame and anger. To move forward, I would either need to alter my values or become completely numb to the pain of dishonoring them. Over time, my pain became so great that I abandoned my beliefs and values. Even though this was all at a subconscious level, there seemed to be no way to repair my shattered values and heart, and I began to shut down. I slipped further and further away from the person God had made me to be. I felt alone. Abandoned. Betrayed. Broken.

My self-loathing and depression grew when I found a pamphlet stored among some old literature at church. It added to my guilt and shame. It described how a "good" Christian teenage girl should act. According to the pamphlet, I had committed a horrible sin. I should not have been alone with a boy. I should not have been alone in a car with him. I should not have kissed him or allowed him to touch me. Those things were all wrong and were all my fault. My sins. Nowhere did it mention that what he did was wrong. It was my fault for being there in the first place.

My interpretation of the pamphlet was that these things were unforgivable. I was convinced that a potential husband and even God himself could not forgive me. I couldn't catch my breath as I read. Every part of my body ached. Because of one night, one moment that I wasn't even completely in control of, I felt that I had become damaged and unforgiveable. If there was any mention of God's redemptive love and grace in that pamphlet, I didn't grasp it. I only felt more guilt, shame, and judgment.

Snapping out of my memories, I found myself back in my room, looking out the window. Intellectually, I had known that these memories would haunt me once I returned home, but I was surprised at how vivid they were and how strong the pain still was after all these years.

I climbed into my old comfortable bed and tried to sleep. The next few days would be difficult, and I would need to be well-rested. Sleep did find me eventually, but it was fretful.

Chapter 7

THE NEXT MORNING, I thought I would check on Grandmother before breakfast. Since her door was still closed, I went downstairs instead. Aunt Lu, of course, was already in the kitchen.

"Is Grandmother awake yet?"

"She was earlier, but she seems to be having a bad day. Oh, don't worry, dear," Aunt Lu said when she saw my concern. "There are good days and bad days. She just needs some rest. I suspect that the excitement of having you here has worn her out a bit. Why don't you help yourself to some breakfast?"

I sat down to what felt like the first true breakfast I'd had in years. Aunt Lu had prepared what my grandfather would have called a real farm breakfast: bacon, scrambled eggs, and biscuits with gravy. I also had several cups of coffee to wash it all down. On a normal day before work, I would just grab some type of breakfast bar as I raced out the door. I was typically at work before the sun was even up, and I never took time to cook for myself at home.

After breakfast, I helped with the dishes. When Aunt Lu went to check on Grandmother and then read the paper, I decided to explore the farm. Exploring the farm usually meant I ended up in the apple orchard, and that was exactly where I found myself today. There was still one tree with a branch low enough that I could hoist myself up and sit in it, and I smiled as I climbed up. Here I was, a grown woman sitting in a tree. I wondered how many times I had done this same thing over the years. Settling into my spot on the branch, I let my thoughts wander and was unsurprised when my past came back to greet me once more.

It wasn't long after The Incident that my boyfriend decided I was no longer good enough for him. After causing what I believed was my damnation, he threw me away. The pain I felt from his abandonment was compounded by the other emotions I was already feeling. I was consumed with guilt and shame, and the only consolation I had allowed myself was the delusion that perhaps we would eventually marry. Now, even that notion had been taken from me. I was Lydia, the girl who had no parents to love her or give her affirmation, and who had been rejected by the first boy she had loved. I felt so broken.

I was also humiliated by the fact that others knew what had happened on our date. And to make matters worse, I worried that word would somehow reach Grandmother. How would she react? Grandmother had zero tolerance for such behavior. She had made her views of premarital sex quite clear.

And what about other consequences? Could I possibly be pregnant? If so, what would I do? I worried myself sick. I felt nauseated anytime I tried to eat, and I told anyone who asked about my lack of appetite that I was just trying to lose a few pounds.

The pain in my stomach was almost as severe as the horrendous pain in my chest. It felt like my heart was going to explode. Breathing normally was a constant challenge. Sleep was fleeting;

it came in short spells. Most of the time, I lay in bed and worried about the *what-ifs*.

My concerns that Grandmother would notice something was wrong were realized when she finally confronted me one morning after I had skipped breakfast again.

"Is something the matter, dear?" she asked, worry evident on her face as she searched my eyes for answers. "You haven't eaten much lately, and you look rather pale. We can pay the doctor a visit today if you're not feeling well."

I did my best to paste on a smile. "I'm fine, Grandmother. Really. Things are just stressful at school."

"Well, you should at least keep your strength up," Grandmother said. She pushed a plate of buttered toast across the table toward me. "You're as thin as a rail!"

"Honestly, Grandmother, I'm not hungry. I've been trying to cut back a little to . . . to lose a few pounds."

Most months, I cursed my cycle. This time, however, I cried for joy when it came. I was so thankful that I wasn't pregnant. Perhaps I could finally forget that this whole horrible experience had occurred.

Chapter 8

I TOOK A DEEP BREATH and shifted my thoughts back to the present. Had I heard someone calling for me? Yes, Aunt Lu was calling from the house.

"Lydia, lunch is ready! Do you want anything?" Aunt Lu yelled.

Had I really sat outside that long? I couldn't remember when I had so completely lost track of time. "I'll be right there, Aunt Lu," I called out.

"You're awfully quiet today. Are you okay?" Aunt Lu asked while we ate our sandwiches.

"Oh yes, I'm fine. I was just thinking about Grandmother," I said. "How's she doing?"

"She's weak today. I took her a little soup. That was all she said she felt like eating. She was sleeping again when I went to get her tray."

"Does she have many days like this?"

"More and more, I'm afraid. Her heart issues cause her to be quite tired."

I still had a hard time reconciling this older version of my grandmother who, not so many years ago, could outwork someone half her age. Another lump formed in my throat at the thought.

To change the subject, I asked, "What work needs to be done around here today?"

Aunt Lu jumped up from the table. "I don't often get offers for help, but I would love some help. My women's group at church is having a bake sale, and I signed up for ten pies and fifty-dozen cookies. I know that sounds like a lot, but the proceeds go to mission work.

I almost regretted the offer. This would be hard work, I knew, and Aunt Lu seemed eager to get to it. She needed help though, so I kept my word. As we rolled out dough and measured cookie ingredients, we talked about several family members I had not seen in years. Aunt Lu told me where they worked, who was recently married, and who had children. She also told me about several neighbors I remembered from my childhood. It was amazing how much had changed in the years I was away. When the cleanup was done, I went to check on Grandmother, but she was still sleeping.

I wasn't used to all the fresh air and the hard way of farm work. I stretched my arm muscles that were fatigued from helping Aunt Lu and went across the hall to relax in my room. The chair I'd moved earlier was still at the window, so I sat down and gazed out at the countryside. It seemed that my past reused to leave me alone, and more memories surfaced the longer I rested. I had hoped that maybe I had moved beyond them altogether, but being here, where the problems had all started, made the memories rise in a powerful way. It was almost as if I was reliving them.

After the pregnancy scare, I had hoped that I could forget the entire experience—but that was not meant to be. Several months passed, and I found myself falling in love with someone new. This time, I told myself, everything would be different. My new boyfriend seemed like such a nice guy at first. In many ways, he was, but he had also heard the stories about me. He was young and wanted to experience life too.

Before I knew it, I was in the same situation all over again. By this point in the relationship, I had convinced myself that I loved him and that he loved me. I gave into his persuasions, but I soon discovered that it wasn't about love at all. And then came the same overwhelming feelings of guilt and shame. I loathed myself. As before, the relationship eventually ended.

I had other boyfriends over the years, and the pattern continued each time: I convinced myself that we were in love and repeated making poor choices. My self-loathing, guilt, and shame grew with each experience, and I was convinced that the only time I felt loved was when I was with a boy.

My family wasn't a physically demonstrative family, and I craved physical touch. I also longed to hear words of love. My family didn't talk about feelings, and we weren't outwardly affectionate. Grandmother always said that true love was shown in how you treated someone, but as a teenager, I didn't understand what she meant by that.

The boys I dated always *told* me they loved me. I never understood until it was too late that words were easy to say, but often more difficult to mean. I certainly didn't understand that honest and complete respect for a person was a large component of real love. My only hope was that each relationship would be different from the one before it.

I didn't realize it was happening at the time, but I continuously presented myself as a victim, so I was continuously victimized. Shame and guilt dictated my actions, and those actions reset the cycle with every new relationship. Perhaps most tragically, because I felt like a victim and didn't feel in control, I thought I had no choices. The only option I could see was whatever was happening to me at any moment. I felt as if I was suffocating, trapped in a life of shame and guilt. In my mind, that was what I thought I deserved.

With each hurt, I shut down a little more and hid behind the wall I built around myself to block out the pain. The main problem with this was that, instead of keeping the pain out, it kept my true friends out and the pain inside. I was all but hidden from the world behind the wall, and my relationships with my family and friends suffered.

I completely shut God out too. How could He possibly forgive me after everything I had done? I kept looking for the one man who would heal my pain. I didn't understand that the healing I needed couldn't come from a person. Once I shut God out, it seemed that I had no one left. I was no longer living my life; I was simply going through the motions.

Around me, everyone knew that something was dreadfully wrong, but no one knew how to help. Even those close to me had no way of knowing the source of my pain or that I was grieving for my shattered self.

Chapter 9

Two YEARS LATER, I had another horrible incident with the first boyfriend. He had been pursuing me again for quite a while. He genuinely seemed to want to have a relationship this time. I questioned whether I should trust him with my heart, but I eventually decided to give him a second chance. My desperate thought was that this was my second chance as well. But once more I repeated the same mistake: I became too serious too soon.

I lay beside him and looked at him, daring to believe that he might say he loved me. Perhaps he would even talk about marriage. I let my mind wander to the future as we lay there together. "I'll wait for you, and we'll get married when you graduate," I wanted him to say. "We'll make a happy, wonderful life together."

But the words I longed for didn't come. In reality, what he said was so dreadful that I couldn't believe he'd said it at first.

"This was a mistake," he said, rolling on his side to look me in the eyes. "It never should have happened. I took advantage of you because I knew you loved me and would have sex with me."

The fantasy I'd created in my mind crumbled in an instant. I couldn't breathe. The displacement of my fantasy with the harsh reality of his words came so suddenly that my heart felt as if it was going to explode. There were no words of love and marriage—

only words of mistakes. I had opened myself up to someone once more, and once again, my heart had been stomped on.

I slipped out of bed without saying a word and got dressed. Was he hoping for a scene? Was he expecting tears? I didn't know, but I would give him the satisfaction of neither. I'd already given him everything else. The only thing I could save myself from at that point was further humiliation.

Since he had driven me to his apartment, I had to ask if he would take me home. It was a long, awkward drive, made to feel even longer because we didn't speak. I stayed numb on the way home, blocking all thoughts of him and the pain that I knew would come. Over time, I had trained my brain to completely shut down so that I would not become emotional in situations like this one. I went directly to my room when I arrived home. There, alone, I was finally free to explore my feelings.

How could I possibly find words to describe my distress? I hurt to the very core of my soul. I had been so sure this time that I'd finally found the love that had eluded me. I hurt so deeply that I wondered if it was possible for a heart to physically break. I knew I couldn't continue to live with this grief. The physical pain was torture, but it couldn't compare to the deep ache in my soul. Perhaps even worse, I believed I was even more of a disappointment to God than to myself.

I had been trying to heal what was broken, but my actions only made it worse. Each time I had been looking for love, I found only pain and agony. In trying to heal my shame on my own, I only created a deeper and more agonizing shame. I had distanced myself from God instead of drawing nearer to Him. I felt the repercussions of my actions stopped me from being able to receive God's grace. I was living a life with no hope.

I knew I couldn't live like this any longer, so I decided that I wouldn't continue living at all. I slipped downstairs to the bathroom, tiptoeing so Grandmother wouldn't hear. When I closed the bathroom door behind me, my anguish washed over me in a giant wave. What little breath I had came in shallow bursts, and the room started to spin. I blinked excessively, trying to focus on something to get my bearings, but it was of no use. The room spun, and I couldn't stand. Suddenly, everything went black. I never felt my head hit the tub.

I learned later that my grandmother came rushing down the stairs when she heard the terrible noise. She saw the light coming from under the closed bathroom door and reached to turn the knob. A terrible feeling ran through her as she realized it was locked.

"Lydia?" she said frantically, but of course there was no answer. She pounded on the door. "Lydia, please, talk to me." She pounded again.

"Where is that blasted key?" Grandmother cried out before remembering it was in a drawer in the kitchen. She ran to find it and then hurried back.

When she finally unlocked the door, she discovered me lying in a pool of blood on the floor. Fear washed over her as she took in the ghastly sight. "No, Lord, please," she said, rushing to my side. It would take an eternity for an ambulance to come this far out in the country, so she called Lu and Vern. When they arrived, together they carried me to the car and raced to the hospital. I regained consciousness on the drive, but the pain was so intense I was not completely aware of what was happening. My first clear memory was the doctor examining me in the emergency room.

The doctor needed several stitches to close the huge gap on the back of my head. Grandmother was beside herself over the whole ordeal. She wondered what had caused me to faint. The doctors ran test after test. There were no drugs or alcohol in my system, and for that, Grandmother was relieved. In fact, they found no physical problems of any kind.

"Ma'am, it's been five days since your granddaughter was admitted, and we've run all the tests we can. They've all come back with normal results," one of the doctors told Grandmother.

"But you still haven't determined why she fainted."

"She most likely suffered from a panic attack and fainted as a result," the doctor said. "In such cases, there's nothing we can physically do for her. I would recommend sending her to counseling."

Grandmother hesitated. She had grown up in a generation where such things as counseling were looked at with a raised eyebrow. Her instincts told her that something was terribly wrong, but she wondered if counseling was the right answer.

The doctors called the hospital psychiatrist, but I sat silently throughout the appointment. There was no chance I was going to admit to strangers what was wrong and why I was depressed. I was not going to admit my sins to them, and I most *definitely* wasn't going to admit that I had considered ending my life. The psychiatrist might be required to tell Grandmother, and that thought upset me even more.

Instead, I retreated even further into myself, more determined than ever to show no emotions of any kind. I didn't want to reveal any part of myself because I was afraid that showing emotions—

sad, angry, or happy—might be a window to my soul. I had been hurt so many times that I couldn't bear to share any more of myself with anyone. It was as if I had become a statue, frozen in expression and emotion.

Grandmother didn't think the psychiatrist was making any progress, so she asked our pastor to talk to me. I overheard them while they were in the hallway outside my room.

"Something is dreadfully wrong. I just know it. Lydia seems even more withdrawn after talking to the psychiatrist," Grandmother told the pastor.

"Has she given any indication of what's going on?" he gently asked.

"Not a word. She barely speaks to anyone."

The pastor was quiet for a moment, thinking the situation over. "If you think I could help, of course I will talk to her."

"I'm sure she won't share anything with you, but I would appreciate if you would try. It doesn't take a trained psychiatrist to see how depressed and withdrawn she is. Perhaps you could just speak to her about suffering and how God could help her with her burdens."

The pastor came in and talked to me, and I wondered if he had ever seen someone hurting as much as me. He spoke of Jesus's love and God's grace. "It doesn't matter what's happened," he told me. "God loves you. He will help share your pain—any pain. God's love and grace are for everyone." He preached and preached.

I listened, but I didn't believe him. What I had done was wrong. It was a sin made worse because I had repeated it over and over, and I knew it was wrong. I felt dead inside. Why should I pretend to be alive?

The shame I felt was so heavy that I couldn't face myself. It was even worse when I thought about turning to God. The guilt was so immense that I no longer tried to pray. I only wanted to hide myself from God. In my mind, I couldn't fathom that God would want to be with me. My shame and isolation were so great that I couldn't believe I was the same as all of God's other children. I decided that I needed no one. I would live totally on my own, by myself, and since I had rejected God, I would live without Him as well.

Chapter 10

I WOKE WITH A START. Had I heard a noise? Instead of covering my head with the pillow like I wanted, I laid there and listened. Then I smiled. How long had it been since I had awakened to the sounds of birds? They were chirping so loudly that I was convinced there was an entire flock of them. I climbed out of bed and looked out the window. Through the early morning light, I saw the silhouettes of two little birds in the tree by my room. All that noise and there were only two of them?

When I looked at the clock and noticed how early it was, I briefly thought about going back to sleep. Instead, I decided to go downstairs. Aunt Lu was already awake and in the kitchen.

"You are certainly an early bird this morning," Aunt Lu said when she saw me. "What are you doing up at this hour?"

"Oh, I'm often up this early," I explained, sitting down in one of the kitchen chairs.

"Yes, but you don't have to go to work. Why are you up?"

"Why are *you* up so early?"

Aunt Lu laughed. "Your daddy used to do that—answer a question with a question. I'm up because your grandmother still wakes up early. I guess it's just part of the farm heritage. I'm getting ready to take her some breakfast."

"I can take that up for you if you'd like."

"Well, that would be fine. Why don't you take some coffee for yourself in case she wants to visit?"

I climbed the stairs slowly, trying not to topple the tray I carried with toast, an over-easy egg, and two mugs of coffee on top of it. I made it to the top without dropping Grandmother's breakfast, but when I sloshed a little coffee, I realized it was a good thing I had never tried to be a waitress.

Hopefully Grandmother won't mind, I thought, knocking gently on her door.

"Come in. I'm awake," she said. Her expression brightened when she saw me. "Well! It's Lydia bringing me my breakfast this morning. What a treat! Come put that tray on the dresser while you help me sit up a bit."

I set the tray down as instructed and then helped Grandmother get situated before handing over her meal.

"I see your aunt put an extra cup of coffee on here. Did she think I was thirsty this morning?" Grandmother winked at me. "I can't believe you are old enough to be drinking coffee."

I picked up my own mug and then sat in Grandmother's rocking chair. "Grandmother, I'm—"

"I know, child, but I still like to think of you as a little girl. Sometimes I even imagine you still being in high school. See, on some days, I think of you as practically an old woman."

"Yes, Grandmother," I said with a smile.

"Lydia," she said, "do you know who I was thinking about the other day?"

"No."

"I was thinking of your high school friend, Claire. Do you ever hear from her?"

"No, Grandmother. I'm afraid I've lost contact with everyone from those days. I've just been so busy at work that I haven't kept up with anyone."

"Oh, I understand, child. I was just wondering how she was. She was such a sweet girl."

"Yes, she was."

Grandmother continued to eat, but she watched me while I sipped my coffee. I don't know what expression I had on my face, but she suddenly asked, "What are you thinking about, child?"

"I'm thinking that farm people sure drink their coffee strong."

Grandmother let out a strong laugh. "I thought you were thinking about the problems of the world. You always look so serious. I'm so glad you ponder such simple things occasionally."

"Actually, I was thinking about how this coffee was a good analogy for the difference between the strong-and-simple farm life versus the complicated life of the city. This is simple, strong, black coffee, but in the city, it can take several minutes to order a single cup. It's never just strong black coffee."

Grandmother laughed even harder. "That's my girl. Even coffee can be a serious matter for you. I suppose that is a good analogy." She shook her head and chuckled before she downed her last sip. Then she grew quiet for a moment. "Lydia, I suppose I'm still a little tired today. Would you take my tray downstairs and let me rest? Maybe this afternoon we could visit a while."

"Of course, Grandmother."

I drained my own mug and then took the tray back to Aunt Lu.

"What's on the work schedule today?" I asked.

"I was going to clean out some of the flower beds," Aunt Lu

said. "I didn't have time in the fall to dig out all the weeds, and they can take over a flowerbed just as soon as you turn your back on them."

"Which flowerbeds? I could clean them out for you. I know it's been years, but I'm sure I can still remember how to pull weeds."

"Why, that would be wonderful," she said. "That way, I can stay in the house in case your grandmother needs me."

Aunt Lu directed me to the flowerbeds in the front of the house. At first glance, I didn't think it would be possible for there to be any weeds left from the fall. They looked like the best-kept flower gardens in the world, but I put down the kneeling cushion anyway and got busy. As I worked, I remembered Grandmother's question. *Do you ever hear from Claire?*

Chapter 11

WHEN SPEAKING WITH COUNSELORS and the pastor didn't help, Grandmother made a desperate attempt to contact the few friends I had. One of those friends, Claire Gordon, was from a devout Christian family. Claire and I weren't that close, but then, I didn't have any of what most people would consider close friends. Grandmother called Claire's mother, who explained that Claire had also mentioned she was concerned about me.

Mrs. Gordon told Grandmother that their family was going to hear a Christian author speak the next week, and she suggested that I join them. "This author really speaks to young women," Mrs. Gordon said. "I've read some of her books, and I think her lecture will be beneficial for my own daughters."

"That sounds wonderful," Grandmother said. "Maybe it will also help Lydia. Besides, it will be good for her to get out of the house and spend some time with her peers."

Grandmother decided not to say anything about the trip until the day before. When I came home from school, she told me that Claire's mother had invited me to go with Claire to hear a speaker. I was suspicious about why Mrs. Gordon had asked me to join them because Claire and I never did things together away from school. She was too perfect, and that reminded me of my own problems. But I was too tired physically, emotionally, and spiritually to fight with Grandmother, so I went.

The presentation was scheduled in a town about an hour away. The long ride was uncomfortable because I only spoke when I was asked a direct question, and even then, I only gave one- or two-word responses. I simply didn't have the energy or the inclination for small talk. We arrived just moments before the lecture began and hurried to find our seats. We had no sooner sat down than the author was introduced on stage.

The author, Joan, started to speak, but it felt more like she began to preach. I desperately wanted to block her out, but for some reason I simply couldn't. I had acquired years of experience with ignoring voices and stifling emotions; it was odd that I couldn't do it on this occasion. Begrudgingly, I listened to her story.

Joan shared about her past. It hadn't been an easy life for her. Her parents were unloving and even abusive. If not for her grandmother, she explained, she might not still be alive. Joan's parents had been involved in drugs and other horrible activities, and her grandmother finally brought her to live with her.

"My grandmother took me to church with her," Joan explained. "At first, I felt unlovable. How could God love me when my own parents couldn't? The example of a heavenly Father brought me no comfort. The only example I'd had of a father was an extremely poor one. When he was high, he would hit me. When he wasn't, he would completely ignore me. Some days, I thought the ignoring was more painful.

"While other girls had mothers who would cook for them or read them stories, my mother hired herself out as a prostitute when she needed more money for her drugs. One of those men raped me when my mother was passed out from her drug of the day. But when I told my mother about it, she said I might as well get used to sex. That was probably how I would have to put food on the table. And since the deed was done, she told me I should get out there and help raise some money for the family.

"I went to school and emotionally fell apart. A kind teacher listened to my story, and together we called the police first and then my grandmother. My grandmother hadn't spoken to my mother for years, and she had never even met me. But she was there to pick me up in just a few hours."

Joan shared that she eventually realized she had two options: one option was to lie on the floor and give up. She could view the things that had happened as life's stumbling blocks, trip over them, and just lie on the ground. In that scenario, she explained, life would never improve. She could accept that she was meant to be a prostitute and a drug user, and she could live in the gutter and wait for death. Or she could move beyond those days and accept option number two. She could choose to view what had happened as a steppingstone to become closer to God. All she had to do was stand on that stone and reach up.

"He is reaching down to take your hand," Joan explained. "Instead of lying in the gutter, you can choose to follow God. You can choose to follow the path that God has planned and that He desires for you. And trust me, God doesn't choose a life in the gutter for any of us. You think your clothes are stained with the blood of sin, but God will wash them clean with the blood of the Lamb. They will be white as snow."

Then she began to sing.

Have you been to Jesus for the cleansing pow'r?
Are you washed in the blood of the Lamb?
Are you fully trusting in His grace this hour?
Are you washed in the blood of the Lamb?

Are you washed in the blood,
In the soul-cleansing blood of the Lamb?
Are your garments spotless? Are they white as snow?
Are you washed in the blood of the Lamb?

Lay aside the garments that are stained with sin,
And be washed in the blood of the Lamb;
There's a fountain flowing for the soul unclean,
Oh, be washed in the blood of the Lamb!

Joan was not a great singer, but no one seemed to care. Her message was sincere, and she sang what she believed. She honestly believed that God would wash away her sins and that God loved her even though her life had been terrible! She had accepted God's salvation, and she would follow His path.

But I quickly decided that there was a major difference between Joan's life and my own: Joan had been placed in those circumstances. She had been born to drug dealers. She had been raped, but she chose not to become a prostitute. I, on the other hand, felt that I had chosen to continue down the road of sin. I had put myself in those situations. What had been a brief relief from my guilt and shame gave way to my view of the truth yet again. In my mind, I still believed that I was condemned. I simply could not acknowledge that redemption was within reach.

I continued down this road over time. People who didn't know me well didn't realize something so dark lived in me. They had no idea about the pain I lived with. Most people thought I was just a serious person. They didn't know my soul ached constantly.

Eventually, even I didn't acknowledge the pain anymore. I just knew that there was no joy in life.

Since I was a good student, I viewed education as an escape from my past, away from my memories and my pain. I received a full scholarship to college. When classes began, I put my head down and studied as hard as I could. Nothing would stop me from running from my past. I would be self-sufficient and not lean on anyone. After college, I received a scholarship to law school. The hours were longer, but I tackled the subjects as I always had. Although I viewed my hard work as a means to be self-sufficient, I was creating artificial core values that I could control. I turned my anger, guilt, and shame into actions to prove and to protect myself. To the outside world, I appeared to be a huge success; but internally, I was as miserable as ever.

Occasionally, I would think about Joan. Could even my sins be forgiven? A seed had been planted in me on the day of Joan's lecture, and it was waiting to be tended. It waited patiently.

I shook the flashback from my mind and looked down at the flowerbed again. I had managed to find a few weeds after all. Once I declared the beds weed-free, I headed over to look at the roses even though they weren't on Aunt Lu's weeding list. They had been my grandfather's passion. I was pleased that, although it had been many years since he had died, his beloved roses were thriving.

My favorite had always been the climbing rose. Someone had taken excellent care of these flowers over time. Though I knew almost nothing about them, I felt drawn to caring for them. I knew that much work was needed to prepare the roses for winter each year. Perhaps I would ask Grandmother and Aunt Lu what needed to be done to continue their wonderful care.

For the first time in a long time, I thought about my grandfather. I had loved him dearly. He had a big, booming laugh that he used often. He just seemed to love life. I could do no wrong in his eyes, and it occurred to me that maybe this explained why Grandmother was always tough on me. I couldn't remember even one time when he had spoken to me sternly. He let Grandmother handle all the discipline.

I wondered about that. Was there a reason for the separation of duties? They'd had a good marriage and were fortunate enough to celebrate fifty years together before Grandfather had a heart attack. I suddenly realized how much I missed him. My parents passed away before I entered kindergarten and then my grandfather when I was in junior high. I had a lot of loss in my life. The grief I felt at my grandfather's death was considerable, but my family didn't discuss difficult emotions.

At the time, I thought I was the only person suffering. Now, looking back, I could see that my grandmother had suffered as well. For many months after Grandfather's death, she had a distant look on her face. It was a look that seemed to say that, while she was physically present, she was emotionally or spiritually absent. I imagine she thought she had to put on a brave front for me, but I wish we could have shared tears and stories.

The flowerbeds lost my attention, and I wandered around the farm, remembering my childhood here. I had not been in the outbuildings for years. Several were still standing on this big farm, but most were not being used now. The barn had always been my favorite, and I walked in and looked around. As a child, I had always been amazed by its size, but now it didn't seem as large as it once had. It was certainly in worse shape than I remembered; in fact, it seemed frail. I wondered how it could stand up to a strong windstorm.

It was certainly different than the senator's barn. A chill ran down my spine as more memories flooded over me.

Chapter 12

I HAD ONLY ONE BOYFRIEND during college, and there had been none since then. Building a career consumed my time. I spent hours at work, forgetting that I had only a few friends, and worked myself to exhaustion. Although I pushed hard to establish myself in a powerful career, I still felt dead inside.

I stayed in casual contact with my grandmother. When I first began working, I phoned home perhaps once a month. The calls were usually strained because she tried to learn about what was happening outside of my time at the office. By that point, I didn't want to discuss anything else. Besides, truthfully, I didn't have much of a life away from my career.

Occasionally I was lonely, but I believed there was less pain with being alone. This meant avoiding having a boyfriend—or any friends, for that matter. I didn't want to talk about this decision because my grandmother always thought I needed to be part of what she called a community, and she would tell me this regularly.

"You need someone with whom you can share the joys and heartaches of life—friends with whom you can spend time," Grandmother would say.

As the calls became more strained between us, they became less frequent. Grandmother would still try to call me at times, but she rarely reached me. I spent most of my time at work, and I didn't take personal calls at the office.

Then, life changed. I met someone.

His name was Andrew, and he was the son of Senator Bishop. I had gained the senator's respect through my dedicated work on issues we both found important. I briefed him on every piece of legislation that impacted his favorite projects. One day, while I was briefing the senator on a piece of proposed legislation, his secretary informed him that Andrew was in the waiting room. The senator invited Andrew in to meet me. The senator explained that he had wanted to introduce us, but Andrew had been out of town for quite some time.

Although there was an immediate attraction between us, I was wary about pursuing any type of relationship. But Andrew was persuasive. He said he found me intriguing and wanted to learn more about me. His calls were relentless. Then, the flowers started arriving. He told me he would continue to interrupt my workday until I agreed to have dinner with him. Finally, partly because I could no longer handle the interruptions, I agreed. I had to admit that I had a wonderful time in his company. He was intelligent and charming. Over time, our relationship grew until we even began to entertain the word *marriage*.

Andrew proposed to me at his father's home. In the barn, to be exact. He had taken me on a tour of the grounds, and I told him how much I loved the barn. I explained that I had been raised on a farm, but I'd never seen a barn so magnificent. He told me that his father was meticulous about the care of his horses, so the stable was exquisite.

While I was admiring the beautiful horses, Andrew dropped to one knee. "Lydia," he said, "this farm is one of my favorite places on earth. The fact that you love it too is proof that you are the woman for me. I've brought other women here, but they always rushed back to the house. You love the same things I love. Will you marry me and make me the happiest man in the world?"

Even though we had discussed our future, I was in shock. I had not allowed myself to believe it would truly happen. With everything I had been through, I never dreamed that being so happy was possible. Tears ran down my face as I accepted his proposal. "Yes, Andrew, I will marry you!"

But soon, the nightmare began. While I was busy planning our wedding, I discovered that he wasn't faithful. He had not one, but many trysts with other women. And he didn't even work that hard at hiding them.

"It's just the way I was raised," he told me when I confronted him about it at my apartment. "My father constantly had a mistress."

"What? That's not possible. I don't believe you!"

"It's true. Just ask him—or even better, ask my mother," he sneered. "Besides, what about it? Just because he has a mistress doesn't make him a horrible man. What's the big deal?"

"He cheated on your mother and broke his wedding vows," I said.

"So?"

"What do you mean, so?"

"That's the way it is. I don't know any man who is one hundred percent faithful to his wife. You need to get used to it."

"Get used to it!" I screamed. "What about the wedding vows? Forsaking all others?"

He laughed. "That's a joke. Those vows are a fantasy."

My mouth dropped open in surprise. "I can't live that way.

I *won't* live that way." I smashed the engagement ring into his hand and pushed him out the door. Then I collapsed on the floor in tears.

After all these years, I thought I had finally found love, acceptance, and approval. Once again, I felt used for someone else's purpose. Every ounce of my energy had been sucked out.

I dragged myself to work the next day even though I was exhausted, because that was what I always did. I worked even longer hours after that so I wouldn't have time to think about another deep, painful loss. That was four years ago, and I haven't looked back since.

I took several deep breaths as I looked around my grandparents' rickety barn. Yes, this barn was a far cry from Andrew's, but it was beautiful too, and it had a wonderful feel to it. Here, I could feel Grandfather's presence.

I had a few short-but-vivid memories of when my grandfather had raised sheep. I must have been incredibly young at the time, but I distinctly remembered how soft the lambs were. Grandfather would bring one over to me and hold the lamb still so I could pet it. This tender memory surprised me with tears.

I also remembered pointing out to Grandfather that the barn would be great for horses. For a while, I thought he might give in. He wanted to; I could see in his eyes. But at his age, he simply couldn't handle the extra work of horses. The idea that my negotiation skills had started early made me chuckle. I also realized that was one of the few times when I had not been successful in meeting a goal.

The longer I was home on the farm, the more memories I had

buried long ago unearthed themselves. I was exhausted from old wounds opening again as I remembered all the long-ago and not-so-long-ago hurts.

I looked at my watch. I had been gone longer than expected, and I thought I should go back to the house before someone began to worry. *What a thought. Someone to worry about me.* I had lived alone for so long, it was odd to think that someone might notice I wasn't around and would worry about me.

Chapter 13

THE NEXT MORNING, Aunt Lu told me that Grandmother wanted to see me. She had been too tired to visit yesterday afternoon but promised we would talk again soon. I was glad to find her feeling better as she invited me in.

"Pull up that desk chair and sit with me a while," Grandmother said when I entered her room.

My heart raced. Though I was an adult, whenever Grandmother asked me to pull up a chair and sit, I still felt like a child. When I was young, these were the times when Grandmother always brought up those hard-to-discuss topics—like why I was so withdrawn.

"I have to say it again," Grandmother said, "I'm so glad you are here, child. I have more on my heart that I need to say. I'm feeling better today, so I better hop to it."

I felt myself starting to shut down. If I didn't, I might not be able to handle this conversation. What else could Grandmother have on her heart? Our last conversation had brought me to the edge, and I refused to break down emotionally.

Of course, Grandmother immediately noticed that my face changed, so she decided to hit it straight on. "You know, you don't always have to be strong. I know I'm dying, and you know I'm dying. It's not a time to be sad. I am old and tired, but my faith

is strong. I know where I'm going. I will see my husband again."
She paused for a moment and studied my face. "And I will see my
precious son and his wife—your parents. I want to tell them how
well you are doing. *Are* you doing well, Lydia?"

"Of course, Grandmother," I said. "I have a great career,
I'm totally self-sufficient, and my health is excellent. I'm doing
extremely well."

She pursed her mouth just like she always did when she
was thinking. She sat for a while without speaking. Then she
proceeded.

"I'm not going to paint a pretty picture or try to figure out
how to reach you, Lydia. I've spent years trying to do that. God
has told me that I must speak plainly with you. What I meant
was, how is your *soul*?"

The question hit me so hard that I felt the wind had been
knocked out of me. No one had ever asked me a question quite
like that, and I didn't know how to respond. I answered honestly.
"I don't know."

Grandmother gently nodded. "Yes, that's what I thought.
I think I have failed you by not speaking so forthright before
now. Lydia, this is the most important question that you could
be asked. You know that old hymn 'It Is Well with My Soul'? It
needs to be well with your soul. Now, the real question is, how
do you get things well with your soul?"

She paused and looked past me off into the distance. "I feel
like rocking. Please help me to my rocking chair. We need to rock
while we talk today."

After she was settled in her rocking chair, she rocked for a
while with a distant look in her eye. I think she wanted to find
the right words, and it appeared that she prayed for quite some

time to find them. Finally, she said, "You see, Lydia, I thought I needed to coddle you."

"Coddle me? You pushed and pushed me!" I took a few deep breaths to calm myself and fought hard to stay in my seat.

Grandmother seemed pleased that I was "alive" enough to react in such a way.

"Yes, I pushed you in school because I knew you were capable. My, you were capable. You soaked up everything like a sponge. Yes, you were bright. Others wanted to baby you because of what you had been through. They wanted to treat you like an antique china doll, but I thought you needed normalcy. Your parents would have pushed you in school, so I did too. I coddled you emotionally and spiritually instead."

Grandmother continued to rock. There was no rushing through her words. She would say what she needed to say when she was ready. I sat, dreading where this conversation was headed as the silence stretched between us. Several minutes passed before Grandmother spoke again.

"I think there are some lessons you still need to learn. These will take time to process. I regret little in my life because regret is a waste, but I do regret this. I should have spoken to you about these things long ago so that I could help you as you take this walk. You will need to cultivate a wise friend to help you because I will not be here."

"But, Grandmother—"

"Hush, child," she said gently. "You need to listen and promise you will think on these things."

I couldn't speak and choked down my desire to scream, but I nodded anyway.

"Lydia, my child, you need to quit hiding behind what has

happened in your life. As I said before, I know losing your parents was difficult. And I don't know what, but I know that there is something more you are hiding from. For years, I have begged God to show me what it was. On this subject, He has been quiet." She chuckled. "I guess I have to turn that one totally over to God. It is hard for your old grandmother not to be able to fix something."

Then she looked at me with a somber expression. "I have never been able to fix you, but God can. You need to quit hiding, child. Quit hiding!

"You see, one thing I have thought about is that perhaps you have been hiding from love. Love can take many forms. It seems to me that you have hidden yourself away from all kinds of love. I suppose some people might call it hiding from affirmation or acceptance. Why would someone—and I am especially thinking of you, my child—hide from such things? Love, affirmation, and acceptance—all humans require these. Why would someone hide from them? How could someone hide from them?"

She paused again before continuing. "You see, child, I believe fear could be considered the opposite of love, or, at least, it can block us from giving and receiving love. I've wondered if fear could be so strong that someone would avoid any chance of feeling or accepting love. But the human need for love is so strong that I wonder how fear could possibly be stronger. All I know is that this fear must be powerful. I wonder, if we hide from or shut out love, do we therefore shut out all other emotions too? Can we feel anything if we shut out love? Emotions are not bad, Lydia. They are not to be hidden from. Emotions are part of being human, and we need to face them. Come to terms with them."

Grandmother glanced at me, as if waiting for me to respond.

When I didn't, she went on. "Do you realize that when you shut out love, you also shut out the opportunity to accept God's love? Of course, I guess that could be the first love that is shut out. People think that they could not possibly earn God's love because of their sins. But that is the point!"

She is really on fire today, I thought, although I didn't interrupt.

"We cannot earn God's love. It is a gift. It is His grace. He loves us no matter what! Not only is there nothing we can do to earn it, but there is nothing we can do to lose it. Do you hear me, child?"

I could only nod and look down at my lap. I knew if I looked at Grandmother, my façade would crumble. I couldn't begin to process all this all at once, so I just sat and listened.

"Here's something else I think about God's love. Blaise Pascal once said that we each have a God-shaped space inside of us. People try to fill this space with a variety of things. Some people try to fill it with money. Some try to fill it with food. Some even try to fill it with drugs and alcohol or power.

"We long to fill this space, but most people don't have a clue or a desire to truly know how to fill it. The truth is, this God-shaped space can only be filled by God. He made us that way. He made us to desire being with Him, but our sins make us think He couldn't bear to be with us. That is wrong! He wants nothing more than to fill that empty space. That is what will make us complete. Let Him fill you, Lydia. Invite Him in. He won't just walk in. Open the door and invite Him in. He is waiting for you. It doesn't matter who you think you are or what you think you've done to offend Him. He is waiting anxiously for that invitation. What are you waiting for, child?"

71

I looked at my grandmother. Where was this strength coming from? These were not the words and the energy of a dying woman. Again, this felt like my grandmother from years ago. I didn't know what to say, so I just sat there, trying to understand what she meant and thinking about how healthy she seemed.

"I've preached you a sermon, haven't I?" Grandmother said, smiling. "I preached to the reverend the other day too. I save my sermons for the people that I love. Do you hear me, child? Do you have any idea how much I love you? That is why I must share these things with you. It is important for you to hear them. I have more to share with you, but now I am tired."

I nodded and stood to leave.

"Before you go, there is one more thing."

With Grandmother, there is always one more thing, I thought.

"I don't want you to rush back to your work after I'm gone. I want you to stay a while and rest. You look so tired. I think it will be important for you to be here. And besides, someone will need to put my affairs in order. Your aunt is weary from caring for me, and I think you would do a better job of this chore. Will you do that for me?"

Grandmother had asked little of me over the last few years. I knew I couldn't say no. "Yes, I will," I answered without hesitation. "But why do you talk this way? You're going to live much longer. Look how feisty you are with me." I smiled.

Grandmother probably would have said it was the first time she had seen me smile sincerely in a long time.

"I saved up my strength for my sermon, child, but I don't know how many days I have left. None of us do. Now, please help me back in the bed. I need to rest for a spell."

After the lecture from Grandmother, I walked around in a daze. I caught Aunt Lu watching me a few times that afternoon, but she never asked me what was wrong. I'm certain I looked distracted. She had known her mother desperately wanted to speak to me about something, but she let me sit with my thoughts and chose not to pry.

I couldn't focus. Grandmother's words replayed over and over in my mind. I sat on the porch for what might have been hours, rocking in a chair, lost in thought. Her words came back in waves—*How is your soul? What are you hiding from? Invite Him in; He is waiting. God loves us all no matter what.* I acknowledged her wisdom. Even when I wanted to deny it, I knew she was a wise woman. Now I acknowledged something more. I trusted my grandmother and her wisdom. I honestly believed she loved me and wanted the best for me, and in that knowledge, I placed my trust.

Grandmother, too, was quiet that afternoon. For her, it appeared that a burden had been lifted. She had said much that she had wanted and needed to. She seemed at peace, but I could see she was also exhausted. It had taken a lot of strength to say what she thought needed to be said. I'm sure she had spent much time in prayer over choosing the right words and even more prayer that I would hear them. God had indeed given her the strength, courage, and words to share with me.

Eventually, I went to check on her. She still looked exhausted, but she said, "Just reflect and ponder, my child. Will you do that?" I agreed and let her rest.

Later that evening, I asked to take some supper to her. I was ready to hear more, and I genuinely wanted to spend time with her.

"I'm too tired to eat just now, child," she told me.

"Did our visit take too much out of you, Grandmother?"

"Well, I'm certainly tired now, but I'm so pleased to have said the things that I did. Oh, and one more thing."

I smiled. "It's always one more thing with you, Grandmother."

"Ah, so it is, but how good it is to see you smile. The one more thing is to remember that you promised me you would stay and take care of things for me."

"Yes, Grandmother, I remember my promise. I will honor it."

"I believe you will. I want you to care for this land. It has been in the family for so long. And I want you to be kind to my farmer. He's such a nice young man, and he has done a good job. Can you do that too, Lydia?"

"Yes, Grandmother, I promise. I'll take care of everything." I leaned over and gently kissed her forehead. "I'll let you rest. Should I come back a little later to see if you're hungry?"

"Yes, dear. That would be nice."

Grandmother smiled faintly as I closed the door behind me. She seemed to notice that there already had been a visible change in me. Things were being stirred up within me, and she could see it. It might only have been a stir, but it was a change nonetheless. Grandmother could always tell when I was thinking.

She heard the sincerity in my voice when I agreed to stay and care for her affairs. There were so many things that would need to be sorted out. Perhaps she had also noticed that the look in my eyes was different too. It was as if a little ice had melted in my soul that afternoon. She had cracked open the door to my soul.

There was much more that I would need to learn, and much healing would be needed, but the door had finally been opened. I'm positive it was with that thought of peace and fulfillment that Grandmother went home to her savior with a smile on her face.

Chapter 14

REVEREND PETERS WAS RECITING the twenty-third Psalm. Why did preachers *always* choose to read that passage at funerals? Wasn't the Bible full of other scriptures that would be appropriate? Wasn't reciting the twenty-third Psalm a little cliché?

"The Lord is my shepherd; I shall not want. He makes me lie down in green pastures; He leads me beside still waters," he said.

Why was it still waters? Why not a raging river? I wanted to jump into a raging river.

"He restores my soul."

I almost jumped out of my seat at that line. At the exact moment that Reverend Peters said *soul*, I felt a jolt like a shock of static electricity. I glanced over at Aunt Lu. No, she hadn't touched me. There was nothing I could see that would've caused a shock. Now that I was fully alert, I gave the pastor my complete attention. The scriptural reading was complete, and he had moved on to his message—a recollection of his relationship with Grandmother and the lessons she had taught him.

He told us Grandmother had once warned him that he'd better not hold anything back when it came time for her funeral. Yes, she had acknowledged it was a funeral, but she said he needed to preach a sermon. He had decided after one particularly meaningful afternoon with her what the theme of his message would be: "God is right here."

"Mrs. Roberts had been communing closely with God one afternoon right before I arrived. I asked how she was doing. 'Oh, just fine,' she answered. 'I'm talking to my Savior.'"

"'You are?' I said, somewhat surprised."

"She looked at me with even more surprise. 'You mean, you don't talk to Jesus?' she asked me, sounding amazed."

"'Well, yes,' I responded, 'but you make it sound like you are talking out loud to your best friend.'"

"'I was,' she told me, still sounding a little surprised. You could tell she was going into her teacher mode. She was going to teach this preacher something."

Those gathered at my grandmother's service nodded. She had taught many of them. If they hadn't been students in her classroom, they had been students in "her world." Grandmother was never pretentious in her desire to teach; she was so natural at it that it simply occurred.

"'You see,' she told me, 'Jesus walks with me every day. When I'm a little lonely, or when I'm happy and I want to share, I just sit down and talk to Him. You see, He's right here,' she said, gesturing to a chair. 'We've just been visiting for a while.'"

"I knew I had to hear more about this, so I pulled up a chair to sit and visit a while myself. I decided I needed to jump in with both feet. 'How is your soul, Mrs. Roberts? Are you ready for the next journey?' I asked."

"'Oh, Reverend, I am ready. I will get to see the prayer warriors who went before me. I suspect my dear friends Agnes and Geneva will be there waiting for me. Don't you agree? And I know my parents and my husband will be there too.' And then, for the first time, she teared up a little as she added, 'Of course, my son and his wife will be there too.'"

"'Those would be Lydia's parents, right?' I asked."

At the mention of my parents, I tensed. I wanted to grab the arms of my chair for support, but I sat unmoving. This sermon was like none I had heard before. It was if the pastor had written it for me alone.

"Mrs. Roberts continued. 'Yes. You know, a mother should never have to bury her own child.'"

"'How did you get through that awful time, Mrs. Roberts?' I asked."

"'Just like now,' she answered. 'Jesus was right beside me. God spoke to my heart. He told me that, for many people, remembering that God is their heavenly Father is a comfort. I told God that I do take comfort in thinking of Him as my heavenly Father, but it wasn't truly meaningful and healing to me at that moment. Then he sent me a beautiful vision. I could see—just like I see you sitting there—Mary kneeling at the foot of the cross. You see, Mary, just like me, had to bury a son. God understood what I was feeling as a mother. He brought me comfort by giving me this vision. God knew. He knew that Mary suffered at the foot of the cross. He knew that I was suffering with my loss too. I knew deep in my soul that He brought Mary through her grief, and He would bring me through my grief too.'"

"She continued on," the reverend explained. "She said, 'You see, in my grief, Jesus was right beside me. I just put my arms out to Him, and He grabbed me and rocked me. Yes, He just pulled me right up, and we sat and rocked. I still had—and still have—times when I grieve, but I knew I could go on. I had to go on,' she said with a smile, 'because He told me to. The walk wasn't always easy. But with Jesus holding my hand, I knew I could do it.'

"'And, you see,' she said, 'Jesus is right here today, just the same as He was then, sitting and talking with me. All you need to do is reach out your hand, and He will take it. Then you can sit down and have a good visit just like I've been having.' She rocked her chair a little and was quiet for a long time."

"Then she said to me, 'Reverend, how is *your* soul today?' I told her my soul was much better just by talking to her and rocking with Jesus. That is the lesson I learned from Leila Roberts. We can all have that kind of relationship with Jesus—that kind of personal and comforting type of relationship. A sit-down-and-have-a-cup-of-coffee-together friendship. But you must reach out your hand. He is right here, waiting for you."

Reverend Peters sat down. He had certainly delivered a powerful and personal message. It appeared that Grandmother had taught him so much, especially about a completely personal relationship with God. I'm sure he would miss those visits with her.

In her beautiful soprano voice, Margaret, the soloist, then began to sing "Turn Your Eyes Upon Jesus." I had always loved Margaret's voice. Margaret had sung in the church choir since I was a little girl. Her voice was so fabulous that I had always wondered why she hadn't tried to sing professionally.

> *Oh soul, are you weary and troubled.*
> *No light in the darkness you see.*
> *There's light for a look at the savior*
> *and life more abundant and free . . .*

I knew this song well. It was one of Grandmother's favorites. When I closed my eyes, in my mind I was a young girl again. I could see Grandmother playing the piano, and I was singing. The song stirred me.

I'd been shocked awake during the reading of the psalm, and the message had brought me to the edge. Yes, my soul was weary and troubled. It was painful to acknowledge, but I had lived in darkness for so long that I couldn't remember ever living in the light. The darkness was everywhere and had been for as long as I could remember. A sad and melancholy child—I knew that was what people had always called me.

Margaret began the hymn's chorus, and suddenly I couldn't stop myself from singing along. Almost before I realized what was happening, my deep alto voice, mellow and soulful, began to fill the room. Most people didn't recognize it, and looked around at each other, trying to determine where the voice came from.

Sitting beside me, Aunt Lu wiped the tears that flowed down her cheeks as she listened to me sing.

I sang on.

> *Turn your eyes upon Jesus.*
> *Look full in his wonderful face.*
> *And the things of earth will grow strangely dim*
> *In the light of his glory and grace.*

The tears that had been threatening to spill out of my eyes for days finally came. Even though I didn't yet truly comprehend what was happening, these tears were for all the ones I had possibly never shed. They were for my parents and my grandfather, for the part of me that had died all those years ago, for the life I had not lived, and yes, for my grandmother. But Grandmother knew. Of course she knew. She was gazing down at me. Even Reverend Peters had a tear in his eye.

God was beginning to touch my soul. A little more of the ice was melting inside me. Grandmother and the reverend had talked and prayed about this very thing. They both knew I had run from God for many years.

Now though, my voice continued through my tears.

> *Through death into life everlasting*
> *He passed, and we followed Him there:*
> *Over us sin no more hath dominion*
> *For more than conquerors we are.*
> *Turn your eyes upon Jesus,*
> *Look full in His wonderful face,*
> *And the things of earth will grow strangely dim,*
> *In the light of His glory and grace.*
> *His word shall not fail you—He promised;*
> *Believe Him and all will be well:*
> *Then go to a world that is dying,*
> *His perfect salvation to tell.*
> *Turn your eyes upon Jesus,*
> *Look full in His wonderful face,*
> *And the things of earth will grow strangely dim,*
> *In the light of His glory and grace.*

Tears rolled down my face. For perhaps the first time in my entire life, I believed. I believed that God's word would not fail me. I believed His promise that all would be well. At this moment, although I didn't fully understand what it meant, I had a new faith. There was a spark in my eyes as I sat looking forward. Aunt Lu handed me a handkerchief. I wasn't surprised that she would be prepared for today. I reached over, patted her knee, and whispered, "Thank you."

Finally, the guests filed out of the church. The family was led out last, and I walked toward the lead car. I wondered whether people noticed that I walked out of the church differently than I had walked in. Aunt Lu told me later that it looked like the weight of the world had been lifted off my shoulders.

Wisely, I had chosen to not drive myself to the funeral. I had no idea that the service would be so emotional, but Aunt Lu had not wanted me to drive. For once, I had bowed to someone else's wishes. A member of the church offered to drive us both to the cemetery. It was a short trip, but it gave me some time to think. What did all this mean? I truly felt that something was different— that I finally believed God's promise that He loved us all. But I wasn't sure of anything else. My head was full of questions and confusion. I wanted to be alone to think, but that wouldn't be a possibility for quite a while yet.

The service at the cemetery was brief, and for that, I was thankful. I hadn't been to the cemetery for many years. Grandmother would now lie next to Grandfather. My parents were buried just to the left of them. Even though I tried to breathe deeply and slowly, my lungs didn't want to cooperate. It was as if my soul wanted to cry out to God. *Help me!*

Suddenly, I felt a kind of peace that I had never felt before. Every cell in my body felt as if warm, soothing water had been poured over me. I was washed in a love that I couldn't begin to describe or understand. I wasn't positive, but I felt that God had somehow blessed me in a way I had never experienced or imagined was possible. Even though I didn't fully comprehend what I was experiencing, I was beginning my faith walk. The path to healing was beginning. I questioned having a religious experience at a cemetery, but then I thought, *I suppose God can choose to speak to you and bless you wherever and whenever He chooses.*

When the graveside service was over, Aunt Lu and I helped each other to the car and went back to the church for a luncheon. Leave it to the women of the church to love us with some food. I thought this church and community were the "eatenest" people I'd ever known. *Here go another couple of pounds*, I thought, glancing at the tables full of my grandmother's favorite dishes. There was fried chicken and spiral-cut ham with a delicious maple syrup glaze. There were also dishes filled with fat-laden party potatoes that had as much cream cheese and sour cream as potatoes. Heaping bowls of green beans and something Grandmother always called "copper pennies" were on the tables too, and I smiled when I saw them, remembering the first time Grandmother had served me the dish. I couldn't believe she was going to make me eat pennies. When I saw them on my plate, I immediately realized they were simply carrots. I asked her why they were called copper pennies. With a wink, she told me that a few extra ingredients and a fun name could make a vegetable more interesting. She was correct. Adding tomato soup, green peppers, and onions, Worcestershire sauce, and plenty of sugar made the carrots much more memorable.

I knew the dessert table would be at the end, and I knew it would be a magnificent sight. Every type of pie imaginable would be on that crowded table. I fondly remembered what my grandfather said about pie. He only liked two kinds of pie, he often told people—hot and cold. It was a wonderful memory.

Years ago, after my grandfather's funeral, I had asked Grandmother about this tradition of gorging after a funeral. Grandmother said it was a time for the family and friends of the deceased to gather and remember them. And some people showed love through food. It was their way of feeding the body as God fed the soul.

But what does food have to do with the soul? I wondered now, just as I wondered then.

If Grandmother was here, she would elbow me and tell me to quit fussing about the why and just enjoy it. Besides, I was holding up the food line. This was the time for fellowship and celebrating. If it brought others joy to do something, and that something was preparing a delicious meal, I shouldn't ask why. I should simply enjoy. I was positive I had actually heard my grandmother saying, "Go enjoy yourself, child. I've gone on to heaven."

Reverend Peters stood to bless the food and all who had labored so we could nourish our bodies. He thanked God for nourishing our souls as well, and he thanked everyone in attendance for coming to celebrate this prayer warrior, this fellow sister in Christ.

"Let us all remember that she has gone home to glory, to be reunited with her loved ones who went before her, and to gaze upon the glory of our heavenly Father. Although we will be sad as we adjust to our lives without her, let us celebrate her life, the wonderful memories we have of her, and the knowledge that someday soon, we will be reunited with her and our glorious savior whom she so eloquently told us is right here. Amen."

I wasn't particularly hungry. Had I done anything except eat since I had come home? *Gone home to glory.* That phrase struck me. In a way, I had come home to glory too, hadn't I? I had experienced an awakening at the funeral, and I desperately wanted to ponder all that had happened. I picked up a plate and mindlessly put some food on it. If I didn't eat something, Aunt Lu would fuss at me that I needed to keep up my strength.

Several people stopped and told me how much they had enjoyed hearing me sing. Some church members mentioned that they remembered me singing alongside my grandmother when I was a child. Others mentioned that they had no idea what a powerful voice I had. Margaret came up and told me that she, too, had enjoyed it. Then, she suggested we sing a duet in church one Sunday.

"I'm so sorry, Margaret. I hope I didn't offend you. I honestly didn't realize that I was singing so loudly," I said.

"Oh, honey, why should you be sorry? That was your soul singing today," she said. "When your soul wants to sing, you have to open your mouth and let it fly. I'm serious that I want to sing with you. Maybe we need to find ourselves a couple more good singers, and we could make a real group."

I laughed. "You're either just messing with me or trying to cheer me up because I made a bigger fool of myself than I realized."

"Nothing of the sort," Margaret said. "Look at me. I really enjoyed how our voices blended, and I think I speak for others when I say everyone enjoyed hearing us. Now, you better keep moving through this line, or people will have something to say to you. They all look pretty hungry."

I finally made it to the dessert table, and I just stopped to stare in awe. Wow! There were more kinds of dessert than I had even imagined. Maybe I was hungry after all. Life was short and unpredictable, and I thought about eating dessert first. Finally, I grabbed a piece of pecan pie and headed for a table.

Aunt Lu followed and joined me at the table. She was keeping a close eye on me. I'm certain that Grandmother had warned her I might take things harder than anyone could predict. My aunt glanced at me again. I wondered if she could tell that I felt more at peace than I had in an exceedingly long time.

While each person was finishing his or her feast, Reverend Peters stood and asked if we should have a short hymn sing.

"We all know that Mrs. Roberts loved to play the piano and sing those old hymns. And she didn't just sing them, did she? No, she sang them for His glory. Janelle, would you come over here and play for us? Margaret, would you lead us in the singing? Lydia, what do you think we should start with?"

I almost choked on my coffee. Could I even remember any hymns? Certainly not when I was put on the spot like this. As I shook my head no, I said, "Whatever Margaret would like to sing would be wonderful, Reverend."

"Lydia," Margaret said, "I seem to remember hearing you and your grandmother sing 'It is Well with My Soul.'"

I nodded. Grandmother did love that one. Margaret started out with her pure voice.

When peace, like a river, attendeth my way,
When sorrows like sea billows roll;
Whatever my lot, thou hast taught me to say,
It is well, it is well with my soul.

I sat and rocked with the music. I had forgotten the words to most of the hymns I had grown up singing in church. But then the chorus came around. I just couldn't help myself, and I felt drawn to join in. Even though I wasn't singing loudly, I'm sure the depth of my voice stood out in the room.

It is well, with my soul,
It is well, it is well with my soul

Something strange welled up inside me. I just wanted to sing.

My sin, oh, the bliss of this glorious thought!
My sin, not in part but the whole,
Is nailed to the cross, and I bear it no more,
Praise the Lord, praise the Lord, O my soul!

Margaret walked over to me and gently touched my arm. She gestured with her head over to the piano. I stood and walked with Margaret as we echoed each other on the chorus.

It is well (it is well), with my soul (with my soul).
It is well, it is well with my soul.

We sang the last verse together.

And, Lord, haste the day when my faith shall be sight,
The clouds be rolled back like a scroll;
The trumpet shall sound, and the Lord shall descend,
Praise the Lord, praise the Lord, oh my soul.

Those gathered in the church hall listened, seemingly

spellbound by the music. Many spontaneously joined in on the last refrain.

It is well, it is well, with my soul, with my soul,
It is well, it is well with my soul.

Reverend Peters leapt up and proclaimed, "Praise the Lord. Amen! Now, this is what I call a hymn sing."

Margaret hugged me, and more tears streamed down my face. I reached for a tissue, but I found none in my pocket. Aunt Lu ran over and gave me a handkerchief again.

"I guess I'm going to need to carry one of these. I don't know what has come over me," I said.

Aunt Lu told me, "The Holy Spirit has opened up your soul. Your soul is shouting out, and it's coming out as tears of joy."

"Tears of joy? Honestly, I'm feeling rather foolish. And I can't believe I was singing out loud again."

"Foolish? That was beautifully sung. Let's sing some more. Your grandmother would say amen to that!" Aunt Lu said.

We continued to sing. I joined in on some songs, but others, I simply couldn't remember. It had been too long.

Finally, people slowly began to gather their things as they needed to continue their day. I looked to Aunt Lu and said, "I think I feel like going too. I'm suddenly tired."

"Yes, child. I think it is time to go."

I quietly chuckled. Even Aunt Lu's tone sounded like Grandmother's.

We went home to what felt like a hollow house.

Chapter 15

AFTER THE FUNERAL, I sat outside as much as possible. I needed to reflect on everything that had happened in the brief time since I had come home. I had faced so much already: remembering past experiences I had desperately tried to bury, having confusing and emotional conversations with Grandmother and dealing with her death, and then having a breakthrough at the funeral. It had been an emotional time, but I felt calmer than I could ever remember. It was a pleasant feeling.

Grandmother's lawyer called just two days after the funeral. He apologized if he was calling too soon, but he thought I might want to get the probate process rolling. I made an appointment to meet him in his office the following day.

Over the phone, he had indicated that Grandmother had left a simple will, and it was. She left money to Aunt Lu, but the bulk of the estate, including the house and the farm, was left to me. This came as a complete shock, and I didn't know how to react. I was astounded to be a landowner and was quite surprised that she hadn't left the land to Aunt Lu, who had lived in the house for many years. Why not leave it to her?

I felt extremely conflicted. Why had Grandmother made these decisions? Did anyone else know the details of her will? Was this her way of pushing me into staying on the farm long-term? Should

I sell it? Should I stay? Should I just leave everything in the capable hands of Aunt Lu and the farmer whom Grandmother had trusted for several years?

I realized that I shouldn't come to conclusions too soon. I needed time to make these decisions. I signed the necessary forms and thanked the lawyer for his time. Then I headed back to *my* farm.

On the way home from my meeting with the lawyer, I wondered if it was time to consider returning to my office in DC. I thought back to what Grandmother had asked me to do: to stay and take care of things. Wasn't that what I had done? The attorney had assured me that Grandmother's estate was proceeding properly. Tomorrow, I would make an appointment to meet with the man who farmed Grandmother's—no, now it was my—land. That was also on my list of promises to keep.

I had fulfilled my obligations, but somehow, I felt that Grandmother had asked for something more. And when I thought about returning to my office, I felt a sense of dread. At any other time when I had been away from work, I rushed to return. I wanted to get back to what I had thought of as positively crucial work. This time, for whatever reason, there was not that same sense of urgency. I had no idea why I felt this way, and that uncertainty added to my confusion. Maybe I would take a few more days and help Aunt Lu handle some other tasks. I still needed to complete some insurance papers anyway, and there was no reason to make Aunt Lu handle all of Grandmother's personal belongings by herself.

The next morning, I told Aunt Lu of my decision to stay a while longer.

She looked up from her coffee cup in surprise. "Are you sure, dear? I'm delighted, but are you sure that is what you want?"

"It just seems like the right thing to do," I said.

Aunt Lu looked relieved and tried unsuccessfully to hold back a smile. "While you're here, then, maybe we could clean up your grandmother's things a little. She wouldn't want her clothes and belongings to collect dust."

I nodded in agreement, but a question still plagued my mind. "Don't you think it would be viewed as—I don't know—cold for us to do that so soon?"

She smiled. "Not at all. Your grandmother would want someone to be able to use those things, not for them to just sit in a closet. Besides, you might need to head back to work at any moment, and I would love the help."

"Yes, of course," I said. "That makes sense."

"Why don't you start on that little desk in her room while I take care of some chores? I'll be up in a while to help you with the clothes."

As I walked up the stairs, I thought to myself that there was something suspicious in Aunt Lu's orders to work on Grandmother's desk. Yes, that was it—they seemed more like orders than suggestions. And she gave them quickly, as if she had been prepared to tell me about the desk all along. That was the odd part. It was as if she had just been waiting for me to announce that I was staying a few more days.

Her suggestion to work on the desk made sense, though. After all, there might be some important papers that had been overlooked. I paused in the doorway before entering Grandmother's room. This was the first time I had been in it since she died. I had tried to go in before, but I lacked the courage.

I took a deep breath and stepped into the room that now seemed somehow hollow without her in it. The faint scent of her perfume still lingered in the air, and when I closed my eyes, I could feel her presence. I could almost see her rocking and smiling as she prayed. I turned to look at her bed and walked over to smooth the covers. I took another deep breath, and then went and sat down at her desk—the desk where she had written countless letters to family members and friends. *Letter writing is such a lost art*, I thought. With fondness, I remembered being on the receiving end of Grandmother's letters. Even though our relationship was sometimes strained, I had always looked forward to those. I felt a prick of heat behind my eyes, and a single tear ran down my cheek as I realized there would be no more letters.

I reached down, opened the larger of the desk drawers, and started to pull things out. There was her box with the stationery in it! Grandmother always had such pretty stationery. Almost all of it had beautiful, embossed flowers along the edges. As I ran my fingers over them, I thought it was sad that people didn't take the time to put their thoughts and feelings down on paper in their own handwriting. It was such a deeply personal way to connect with someone.

Next, I pulled out a simple-but-lovely journal. This find surprised me because I had never known my grandmother to keep a journal. I wondered if I should open it. It seemed an invasion of her privacy, but after an internal debate, I decided to see if it was important. If it was a private journal, as it appeared, I would set it aside and ask Aunt Lu about what to do with it.

When I opened it, however, I was shocked to see the title on the top of the first page: "Lessons for Lydia." I read on, at first with a little guilt, but then quickly realizing this must have been intended for me.

My dear child,

There are so many things on my heart that I feel I must share with you, but I am afraid that I won't be able to do so in person. My heart is fading, and my days here are short. I continually pray that you will come home. I know you say you are busy with your career. However, I believe you are busy trying to prove something to yourself, though I'm not sure what. Perhaps you are just running.

I don't know if you are running from your family or this farm or your past, but, my child, I so desperately miss you and wish I had time to tell you so many things. I have decided to write down my thoughts so that perhaps you will read this and reflect on them. You will need time to ponder the things I will write. They cannot be discerned quickly or easily. Promise me that you will take the time to ponder what I am going to share.

I stopped reading. As I quickly flipped through the pages, I couldn't believe Grandmother had written all of this for me. This journal came as a complete shock. Why hadn't she told me about these things before? Of course, I admitted to myself, when could she have done so? My career had preoccupied me for years. Then I reminded myself that I'd had to be focused on my career because I had no one else to lean on.

I immediately realized I was rationalizing and that I could have taken time off to come home if I'd wanted to. It wasn't as though my grandmother's poor health was a shock. She had been in her nineties. I felt a wave of grief come over me—for the grandmother I had lost and even more for the relationship I had ignored. I was forced to acknowledge that I had been self-absorbed and had shut everyone out of my life.

I turned my focus back to the journal. The next entry shocked me because it touched on that very topic.

My child,

You cannot live this life alone. While you should know that I am the last person to think a woman needs a husband to be happy, I do have to wonder why you have never really had a steady, serious relationship. At least, you have not mentioned one to me.

I stopped reading again because I felt even more remorse. I had never told my grandmother about my brief engagement. Perhaps I'd had a premonition that it would not last, but that was no excuse from shutting her out of my life as I had in the last few years. I blinked away more tears than I could count, took a deep breath, and continued.

You have also never mentioned talking to or going anywhere with friends.

You will need friends as you discern your path— perhaps a mentor. Perhaps even a pastor or a wise friend who has already done some discernment in his or her life and path. It is good to have someone to discuss challenging topics with and to raise thought to challenging ideas.

You need friends, Lydia, and I'm talking about a soul friend, not just a surface friend. A friend with whom you

*can discuss anything and everything, including your fears
and dreams. I challenge you to think on this and open
your heart to this idea. The topics in this journal will be
easier to digest if you can share them with someone.*

I put the journal down. I supposed my grandmother had
many friends, but I wondered who her soul friends had been. I
smiled as I thought about her. It was completely appropriate that
Grandmother was teaching from the Great Beyond. If ever there
was a woman who could and would teach after death, it was my
grandmother.

Aunt Lu called up the stairs. "Sam is here to see you, Lydia."

"On my way, Aunt Lu," I replied, closing the journal and
putting it back where I'd found it.

Samuel Harmon had been Grandmother's farmer for several
years. He was a few years older than me, but I remembered him
well. We had ridden the school bus together. I always thought you
could learn quite a bit on a school bus if you simply sat back and
observed. I remembered that he was extremely quiet and polite. I
was not surprised he became a farmer; he always preferred to be
outside working with his hands instead of being in school.

"Would you like to come in and sit down, Sam?" I asked as I
joined him in the entryway.

"No thanks," he said. "I'd rather talk outside. I'm a little
dirty, and I don't want to track in any mud."

We stepped out onto the porch and closed the door behind
us. "Sorry about your grandmother, Lydia. She was an amazing
woman."

"Thank you. I'm continuing to learn how amazing she was."

There was an awkward silence between us for a minute, and Sam shifted his weight from one foot to the other. He cleared his throat nervously and shoved his hands into his pockets before speaking again.

"Look, um, word is that you now own all the land."

I smiled. "You certainly don't beat around the bush. Yes, Grandmother left the land to me."

"I'm just, uh, wondering if you are planning any, um, major changes."

"No, I'm not. Obviously, I know nothing about farming. Even when I lived here, I guess I never paid any attention. Grandmother told me about what a wonderful job you've been doing, and she trusted you completely. I would be thrilled if you'd just keep doing exactly what you've been doing."

Sam slowly exhaled a sigh of relief. "Thank you, Lydia. I really appreciate it. And I thank you for sharing your grandmother's words with me. Like I said, she was an amazing woman." Silence fell between us for a moment before he spoke again. "How long are you staying?"

"Are you hoping I'm leaving soon?" I flashed him a grin.

"No, no, nothing like that." He ducked his head slightly as his cheeks flushed. "I didn't mean anything by it. I figured you'd want to get back to your work. You haven't spent much time here in recent years. I assumed you would need to get back."

"I'm sorry," I said. "I was just teasing you a bit. I know people are probably shocked I'm still here. I want to help get everything in order before I leave. There's so much work on a farm, and I guess I had forgotten that." I glanced around. "I'd also forgotten how peaceful and beautiful it is."

I studied Sam as I spoke. He had probably been worried that I might have other plans for the farm or heard rumors that I might even want to sell. It wasn't in his personality to come right out and ask things bluntly like he just had, but the dark circles under his eyes made me wonder if he had lost sleep over it. He looked like a huge weight had been lifted now that he knew I was going to let him keep farming.

"I need to get back to my work, Lydia, but I just have to say thank you again."

"No, Sam, thank you. I honestly don't know what I would do if you weren't taking care of the farm. I might even want to learn a little more if you'd be willing to help me. I probably should know something about the farming world if I'm going to own some land."

"I can come back tomorrow and go over a few details of the arrangements your grandmother and I had."

"That would be great. What time would work best for you?"

He smiled sheepishly and said, "How about nine o'clock? I sure would love some of your aunt's baked goods."

I laughed and told him nine would work well. He looked like he might want to ask me something else, but he didn't say anything. He simply shook my hand and told me that he'd see me tomorrow.

I was grateful that someone my grandmother had trusted oversaw the farm. I was also pleased that I could mark something off my to-do list. Another task had been accomplished.

The next morning, I ate a light breakfast with the plan that I would enjoy some coffee cake while Sam and I talked. When Aunt

Lu learned that Sam was coming, she went on one of her baking sprees. The entire house smelled delicious, and my stomach began to growl.

I greeted Sam at the door after he arrived. "You will not be disappointed this morning with your midmorning break options," I told him. "Aunt Lu has been busy baking three coffee cakes. Would you like a piece of cinnamon, blueberry, or cream cheese?"

Sam replied, "Yes, please."

At first I was confused, but then I understood. "I'm guessing that means a piece of each."

"It sure does. Where's Lu? I want to thank her properly."

"She's in the living room reading the paper."

"Okay. I will stop in there before I leave. Are you ready to go over the arrangement your grandmother and I had?"

"Yes. And I have paper and a pen so I can take notes."

Sam gave me the papers that Grandmother's lawyer had drafted, and he explained the details to me. We agreed to leave everything the same for another year. Then, we would reevaluate to see if we both wanted to continue. He had also begun trying to explain the agriculture world to me. I picked up on most of the details, but I was relieved to have Sam in charge of the farming.

When we were done going over the agreement, we both sat and lingered over our coffee. I felt at ease sitting there with Sam. There were not many people I could say that about. Eventually Sam pushed his chair back, said he needed to get back to work, and stopped to thank Lu for the coffee cake on his way out. I said goodbye to him and then went back to clean up the kitchen. I felt we'd had a good meeting, and it seemed that Sam was pleased as well.

Chapter 16

ON SUNDAY AFTER THE FUNERAL, Aunt Lu asked me if I would like to join her at church. Although I hadn't attended in years, I thought I should go. Truthfully, I felt drawn to it.

Since it was the first time that I had been to the church after the funeral, many of the members came to speak to me. This church really was a family. Many of the members had known each other for years. It was quite likely that their parents—and maybe even their grandparents—had known each other too. It was radically different from the life I knew in the city, where you usually didn't even know your next-door neighbors. It was a nice feeling to go somewhere everyone knew me.

Of course, there were some definite negatives to that as well. If someone made a poor choice, everyone in town knew about it thanks to the rumor mill. They would know what the person had done and the punishment he or she had received. *People probably still remember what trouble my parents had been in as children,* I thought.

Though I was nervous about this first time to church, I found comfort when so many people inquired as to how Aunt Lu and I were doing. I'm certain many of them also wondered how long it would be before I took off again, but they kept that to themselves. After the service, when everyone was enjoying coffee and donuts,

Mrs. Stephens, one of my grandmother's close friends, asked the question.

"How long do you plan to stay with us, Lydia?"

I smiled and decided to answer honestly. "I'm not sure, Mrs. Stephens. There are so many things to do, and I'm not sure Aunt Lu can handle it all." Then I teasingly asked, "Are you hoping to get rid of me soon?"

"Oh, you little devil. Of course not," Mrs. Stephens said, playfully patting me on the shoulder. "I know this must be a rather boring life compared to the one you have been living. I just supposed you were anxious to get back. You know we would all love nothing better than to have you stay here permanently. It was your grandmother's fervent prayer that you might one day consider that."

I was taken by surprise. "Really?"

"Oh yes. She must have felt that you were putting too much pressure on yourself and that it wasn't healthy. Her hope was that one day you might see the beauty in a simpler life. A more reflective life, I believe she used to say. I don't think she thought that was possible with your life in the city."

"To be honest, I think I'm seeing a glimpse of that. I haven't made any permanent decisions, but I'm not feeling a strong desire to go back right now. I'll certainly stay at least until I can get on top of things and make sure Aunt Lu will be okay."

Mrs. Stephens put her arm around me. "I think that is an incredibly wise decision. Take your time. This is a perfect opportunity to reevaluate your priorities and your life."

I sipped my coffee as Mrs. Stephens walked on to greet another neighbor. *What an interesting exchange!* I thought. I couldn't remember ever having a discussion with anyone here where I had been treated as an adult. Then I realized that, just as I hadn't allowed for adult conversations with my family, I hadn't allowed for them with church members either. I always rushed in, did the obligatory church service, and hit the road again. There was never time to give anyone a chance to have a meaningful conversation.

As I was thinking about this, a young woman whom I didn't recognize walked up.

"Are you Mrs. Roberts's granddaughter?" she asked.

"Yes, I'm Lydia."

"Hi. I'm Gail Hinthorne." She extended her hand for me to shake it. "I teach history at the high school. Do you have a minute?"

"Certainly. It's nice to meet you, Gail. Have you lived here long?"

She smiled. "By this community's standards, not at all. I've only been here about three years."

"You're absolutely right," I said, chuckling. "You need to live here about fifty years before you're not considered new to the area. What can I do for you?"

"Well, like I said, I teach history at the high school. I understand you're an attorney and have worked in government in Washington, DC. I was wondering if you would be willing to come speak to my students. I like to present material in a variety of ways, and I thought having you share with them might make some of the governmental and political information come to life."

"I might have to clean it up a bit for the high school level," I admitted.

Gail chuckled. "Well, we'd want it to be the PG version."

"Don't you think I would bore them to death?"

"Not at all. First-person accounts are always more interesting than a lecture. You could give them some personal information about the sights and sounds and people of the capitol."

I had to smile. "You seem so passionate about teaching. I'd be honored to speak to them, but I'd like to sit down with you beforehand and find out a little more about what topics you'd like me to cover."

"Oh, Lydia, this is fantastic! I've been struggling to make this unit a little more interesting, and you are exactly what I've been praying for. Could we sit down to talk next week?"

"Now, wait a minute." I laughed. "Me, an answer to a prayer and interesting too? I'm not sure I'll be able to live up to this."

Gail touched my arm and looked me right in the eye. "Yes, you will. I just know it. I'll be in touch."

With that, Gail left—or rather, more like she bounced out of the church. I shook my head. I was shocked to meet someone who was so passionate about her work, and Gail's enthusiasm surprised me.

After a fabulous Sunday dinner at the farmhouse, I excused myself after all the dishes were finished. There hadn't been much time to read Grandmother's journal since her funeral, and I was anxious to return to it. *Is it my grandmother's, or is it mine?* I wondered.

I made myself comfortable in her favorite rocking chair and pulled the journal out of the desk drawer where I had left it. In a way, I still felt that I was trespassing even though the journal had clearly been written for me. Did Aunt Lu know Grandmother had written this?

The next section in the book appeared to be daunting. It read,

"The Cross." I breathed deeply to prepare for what I guessed would be a rather serious section.

You must take up your cross and follow Jesus. Lydia, my dear, we have heard this time and time again, haven't we? What does it mean to pick up your cross and follow Jesus? I'm sure it means different things to different people. To me, Christ's purpose was the cross. He was sent here to die on it. Not in vain, of course, but for our sins. My belief is that God sends us all to Earth with a purpose. It is my opinion—and yes, others may believe this phrase means something completely different—that picking up your cross is following God's divine purpose for you. If your purpose is to be a teacher, like I was, then you pick up that purpose and follow God by being a teacher. So, no, it is not a literal cross. That was Jesus's divine purpose.

We all have a purpose, Lydia. What is yours? I do not know. That is for God to share with you. I see so many gifts in you, and I know that God could call you to do many things. It was probably a bit easier for me. Teaching was what I was good at. It brought me such joy.

I just see so many talents in you, Lydia. Probably talents that you do not see. To make this subject more confusing, I'm afraid, is that sometimes our purpose is more about being than doing. I will come back to this topic later.

How I wish I could be with you to help you walk this path and discover your cross, your purpose. It was not meant to be. That is why it is important for you to find a "soul friend" with whom you can discuss this crucial topic. The path may seem confusing at times, and it is good to walk it with a friend.

God will reveal His divine purpose for you, because that is why He has given you your own set of special talents. You will need to pray—and most importantly, listen—during this time, but I know that God will show you the path.

I have prayed for discernment for you. You will need to be aware of how you know when it is God speaking to you. For me, I just have such a peace when God has spoken to me that I know the message has come from Him. You must be still and listen. Do you remember what I always told you when you were little? God gave us two ears but only one mouth. We must listen twice as much as we talk. Be still and know that He is with you and that He will reveal not only Himself but also His purpose for you. What a journey it will be!

I realized I hadn't taken a breath the entire time I read this entry. It was such a serious topic that I had to reread it to grasp Grandmother's message. I wished that she had told me about these things in person, but I also realized that I hadn't been ready to hear them before now. Now the timing was right for me to learn these lessons.

My eyes filled with tears again. For someone who had never allowed herself to cry, I certainly had been crying a lot lately. I allowed myself these tears, and although I wasn't completely certain about Grandmother's entire message, I knew this was not only an important lesson but also an important revelation concerning my path for the future. A purpose. A purpose for my life. Chills ran through my body.

The sound of tires on the gravel caught my attention. I glanced out the window to find Sam's pickup pulling up to the house. I hadn't planned on seeing Sam today, and I didn't think he generally worked on Sundays. I was concerned that something must be wrong, so I headed downstairs to meet him.

Aunt Lu beat me to the front door and greeted him as she did most people. "Come in, Sam. Would you like some coffee and maybe some dessert?"

"Well, sure, ma'am, if it's not too much trouble," he said. Then, turning to me, he said, "Hello, Lydia. Do you have a minute?"

"Sure. Would you like to sit down?" I gestured to the dining room.

"I'm more of a sit-in-the-kitchen-type person, if you don't mind."

"Of course. Let me help Aunt Lu with some coffee. Come on in and have a seat."

Aunt Lu served some of her famous chocolate pie, offering both Sam and me a piece. I declined this time, which made Aunt Lu ask if I was feeling all right.

"Aunt Lu, I'm going to gain a hundred pounds if I keep eating like this. I've got to cut back a bit," I said.

"Well, I sure do appreciate it, Lu," Sam said. "I'm not so worried about my figure." He grinned, and I found myself blushing. I didn't think I'd ever really seen Sam smile like that. I felt a little embarrassed for some reason, and I hoped Sam didn't notice.

After he'd taken a few bites, he got down to business. "I was going through some mail, and I found some papers that need to be signed. I apologize for bringing them on Sunday, but with, well, everything that's happened, I hadn't gone through them yet. We need to get these taken care of soon and get them to the insurance company." He pushed the papers my way across the table. "I signed them already, but you'll also need to. Do you mind mailing them after you've added your signature?"

"No, not at all," I said. "I can take care of that."

He nodded his thanks and then turned his attention to my aunt. "Thank you so much for the pie, Lu. It sure hit the spot. I guess I better move along."

"Thanks for stopping by. I'll take care of these forms tomorrow," I said.

"Umm . . . thanks, Lydia." He hesitated for a moment, as if he wanted to say something more, but then thought better of it and made his way out before I could ask what was on his mind.

His behavior seemed peculiar, so I decided to ask an expert about it. "Aunt Lu," I said, "does Sam often stop over like that?"

"Oh, now and then. I've always thought he had a nose for when I was in a pie-baking mood. Why do you ask?"

"Well, he seemed like he had more on his mind than this paperwork, but he left so abruptly. I was simply curious."

"I'm guessing he was just hungry for some good dessert."

"Oh, okay," I said absently.

"You all right, dear?"

"Hmm?" I said, distracted. "Oh, yes, I'm fine. Like I said, I was curious."

Aunt Lu studied my face for a moment while I tried to keep my expression as neutral as possible. Thankfully, the phone rang, and she jumped to answer. "Hello? Oh yes, dear, she's sitting right here." She pulled the phone away from her ear, her hand covering the receiver. "Lydia, it's Gail." She held out the phone to me.

I smiled as I took the phone. "Hi, Gail, how are you?"

"I was so excited after we talked that I just couldn't wait to talk about what I had in mind." The young woman's enthusiasm was obvious even over the phone, and I laughed.

"You might be the most passionate teacher I've ever met," I said.

"I confess, I'm guilty. I love my job! I was wondering if you'd like to meet me at the school for lunch one day this week. I'll even buy you a school lunch."

"Well, I've been thinking that I need more adventure in my life, but I'm just not sure I'm ready for that adventure. Why don't I bring something for us to eat instead? You know I live with the best cook in the county."

Aunt Lu chimed in. "Who is that, dear?"

I smiled. "Aunt Lu, you know it's you. Would you mind helping me make something for lunch for Gail and me?"

"Oh, I'd be delighted."

"Okay. Gail, did you hear all of that?" I said, putting the receiver up to my mouth again.

"Just that you are trying to sweet-talk your aunt into fixing us some lunch," Gail said.

"Oh, I'll help too," I explained. "I'm a great assistant. What day are you thinking?"

"Are you free on Tuesday? I have lunch at eleven thirty. I only have forty minutes, so we'll have to talk fast. Or, rather, I'll have to talk fast, and you'll need to listen fast. Will that work?"

"That should work. I'll see you Tuesday."

I filled Aunt Lu in on the lunch plans after I hung up the phone. She smiled and told me what a nice woman Gail was.

"I'm glad you have found someone your age to get to know while you are home. You might discover that you and Gail have a lot in common."

Chapter 17

ON TUESDAY MORNING, I helped Aunt Lu prepare the food for my lunch with Gail.

"Maybe I should eat the school lunch after all. I haven't had much adventure for a while."

"Nonsense," Aunt Lu said. "That sweet young woman doesn't eat enough. She needs more than just *one* of my home-cooked meals. And I think you have had plenty of adventure. You inherited a farm. I call that adventure."

"Aunt Lu, I've been wondering about that. Umm . . . well . . ."

"Spit it out, child. I've never known you not to be able to find the words you want."

"Are you okay with Grandmother leaving the farm to me? It just doesn't seem right."

Aunt Lu smiled and pulled out a chair. "Come over here and sit. It's absolutely the right thing. Your grandmother and I discussed it many times. I want to stay here as long as I can, but I don't want the responsibilities. I'm not getting any younger. I'd like a slower pace. Taking care of the garden is all the responsibility I want. The whole farm? No, thank you."

I sighed in relief. "That's a weight lifted. Grandmother's will surprised me, and I was worried it may have surprised you, too, or even have been hurtful."

"Not at all, dear. This was decided quite some time ago. It is what your grandmother and I both wanted." She patted me on the shoulder as she turned back to the meal she'd prepared. "Now, we need to hurry and finish packing this food! You don't want to be late."

I eyed the spread before us and chuckled. "You know, Aunt Lu, there are only going to be two of us. There must be enough food for ten or twelve people here!"

"There are other teachers at the school who might want something to eat. Now you can share."

"I'll probably be accused of trying to bribe a teacher, but okay."

I wasn't sure I could carry all the food in just one trip. I felt a little like Santa Claus carrying all his Christmas packages. After struggling to open the doors with completely full hands, I met Gail in the main office. Her eyes grew wide at the sight of the load in my arms.

"Good grief, did your aunt think she was cooking for the whole school?"

"She insisted I bring all of this, and we are supposed to share it."

"I was hoping she didn't think that just the two of us could eat this much." Gail paused for a beat as she surveyed all the food. "Well, maybe we shouldn't share the pie right away. Let's take the rest of the food to the lounge. We can fill our plates there and then go to my room to talk."

Walking down the halls of my old school transported me back to when I was a student. More memories, some happy, some not-so-happy, flooded back. I took a deep breath and kept walking. The walls were still painted the same institutional gray. The lockers were the same too. Even the large group pictures of every graduating class since the school opened still lined the walls. I wondered if I would know any of the current teachers. Perhaps I had been gone so long that they had retired or moved on to other schools.

That question was answered as soon as Gail opened the door to the lounge. My beloved English teacher, Mr. Carroll, was just sitting down.

I couldn't help but smile. I put the food down on a table and said, "Mr. Carroll, I don't know if you remember me, but—"

"Lydia! Of course!" he said, interrupting me as he jumped to his feet. "How could any teacher forget you? I was so sorry to hear about your grandmother. I'm afraid I was out of town and couldn't make the service. How are you doing?"

"I'm fine."

"And your aunt Lu?"

"She is actually doing quite well, but I don't think she knows what to do with her time. When Gail invited me to come and meet with her today, Aunt Lu insisted I bring all this food. She wanted me to share with everyone."

Mr. Carroll smiled. "It's most appreciated. Since you're here on official business with our fine history teacher, I won't keep you. But will you promise to come back and visit me? We won't tell Lu, so she won't work herself to death."

"I'd enjoy visiting with you very much. Shall I contact you here to find a good time?"

"That would be good, yes. And, Lydia?"

"Yes?"

"It's so good to see you."

After filling our plates, I followed Gail to her classroom. I smiled as I looked around. My love of history and government had blossomed here. I could almost hear the voices from my past as I walked around the room. On many occasions, I had debated with my history teacher about various topics.

"Hello, Lydia? Are you listening to a private conversation?" Gail asked, breaking into my thoughts.

"Oh, I'm sorry, Gail. I was just remembering being a student in this room. This was where I decided I wanted to be a lawyer. I'm back in the present now."

Gail smiled. "I think this is going to be great."

"I just hope I don't disappoint you or bore your students. What exactly are you looking for?"

"I would love for you to bring the Constitution to life. Specifically, I would love for you to bring our three branches of government to life."

"I can see you don't want much," I said, winking at Gail.

"I think it will be easy for you. What happened in this room obviously made an impact on you. Bring that energy and those memories to life."

I smiled. "I guess I could try."

"What really speaks to the kids are personal stories and anecdotes—not just about how things are supposed to happen, but how they really happen. Stories about the people you have met and worked with. For example, what have you encountered in your years working in and around government? Not just what is written on paper, but the real, everyday stories. That's what makes it come alive."

"They'll probably be sickened if I tell them how it really works."

"Okay, well, perhaps you shouldn't include the really gory stories."

I thought for a few moments. Could I really do this? "I think I can tell them about a few things without making them ill or getting myself in trouble."

"Yes!" Gail exclaimed. "That's what I want to hear. Now, let's eat. I'm starving."

My mind raced with ideas about what to share and how to share it. I never thought I would be a teacher, but I guessed I could try it for a day.

Chapter 18

WHEN I ARRIVED HOME AFTER my meeting with Gail, I told Aunt Lu that I needed to go upstairs to rest for a while. "I ate so much, I have to rest and let it digest. I swear you are trying to fatten me up for the market or something."

"Oh, nothing of the sort," Aunt Lu said. "I just don't think you've eaten healthy for a long time."

I moaned when I moved and said, "Yes, well, do we need to make up for several years in just a few weeks? I may not survive."

"Yes, dear, I hear you. Go rest a bit." Aunt Lu waved her hand to dismiss me to my room.

When I made it to the top of the stairs, I decided to go sit in Grandmother's room. I sat in her rocking chair and pulled the journal out of her desk, flipping it open to where I'd left off. The next section was entitled "Prayer."

> *Perhaps I should have started with prayer. This is where your walk with God must begin. People have misconceptions of what prayer is, or rather, what it should be. I do not believe that God puts parameters and constraints on prayer. I think He will meet us anyplace and anytime we want to meet Him. He hungers to visit with us. Yes, I said "visit."*

I don't think you should limit yourself to thinking only about some formal version of praying. Praying is simply visiting with God—just like two friends sitting down and catching up. I like to pray in my rocking chair. It puts me in a visiting mood. I just rock and listen and rock and talk. Notice that I put listen *first. I think that is another mistake people make.*

Prayer is not just a time to tell God what we want or what we fear. No, I think it is more important to spend time listening. Remember—two ears but only one mouth. More time should be spent listening. With the world as loud and busy as it is, we often don't take time to listen to God—or to anyone, for that matter. You may need to practice praying or, perhaps better put, you may need to practice listening.

If I may challenge you, Lydia, this is what I would suggest: sit someplace where you can be comfortable. Feel free to use my rocking chair. Sit quietly. Then ask God, what would you have me learn today? Or what do I need to hear from you today, God? Practice listening to Him.

Another question people have is, how do I know if what I hear is from God? As I mentioned in another entry: for me, I always have an other-worldly sense of peace when I hear from God. I feel at peace from the top of my head all the way to my toes. Every part of my being is at peace, and I sense a comforting and knowing "yes." You may have to practice so that you will be able to recognize the feeling that God will give to you.

As you begin your prayer journey, you may find it necessary to be in a quiet place. By this, I mean being in a quiet place in your soul as well as in your surroundings. As you gain experience, your surroundings may not need to be as quiet, but I do believe your soul will always need to be in a quiet place to truly hear God's words for you.

You may notice that I have used the word practice *several times. I do believe that when you are doing something new, you often must practice until it feels comfortable. As with many new activities, how you get started on a new task is not as important as simply beginning it. This is my advice to you: just pray! This is the only way I know to truly visit with God—the only way to learn about God's calling for us. The only way to learn about the divine purpose that you have been given.*

Love, with much prayer,
Grandmother

I sat and thought through these new ideas about prayer. *Practice praying.* That was a new concept for me. I liked Grandmother's perspective that a person didn't have to be so proper in how to pray. That certainly took some pressure off the process.

I was so intrigued with the lesson that I continued reading.

No Matter What

My dearest Lydia,

I'm quite tired today, but I keep feeling called to write for just a bit. One of my many prayers—but perhaps my most important—for you is that you might know how much God loves you. In fact, He loves you no matter what. It does not matter how imperfect we are or how small or large our sins; God loves us. It does not matter that our actions sometimes disappoint God. His love will still hold us close. He longs to draw us close to Him. When we feel alone, He is with us. When we feel unlovable, He loves us no matter what. He is there. Our Father, our friend, our savior. Think about what that truly means. No matter what, He loves us. No matter what, He has saved us. No matter what, heaven awaits us because of His grace. There is nothing we can do or fail to do that will change this. Even when we feel like running away from God, His grace means that His love will never leave us.

Amen!

As always, Grandmother's journal entries left me exhausted. I had even more to ponder and process. Now, I really did need that nap.

Chapter 19

My PRESENTATION TO GAIL'S CLASS appeared to be a success. As I prepared, it didn't take long to realize that this couldn't be a lecture for them. The students needed to be involved to keep them interested. I asked them many questions and cited many current news items. To make the material more interesting, I tried finding ways to relate to them and their interests. The students responded with great enthusiasm. It helped that I pointed out that I had thought about preparing a lecture. They groaned at that, so I knew I was on the right track. The conversations were still in progress when the bell rang, and Gail practically had to kick them out of the classroom so they would go to their next classes on time.

When we were finally alone, Gail said, "Thanks a lot."

I was taken aback. "That sounded a little sarcastic. Was I that bad?"

"No! You were that good. They won't want me to teach anymore. I may have just lost my job."

Gail smiled at that, and I finally realized she was joking.

"Oh, you had me going," I said. "I thought you were upset or that I was horrible."

"No, you were fabulous. Thank you so much! The questions they asked showed that they really connected to you and understood what you were saying. I saw light-bulb moments as if they were finally understanding that this is current, not just ancient history. I cannot thank you enough. And, if you ever decide to take up teaching as a career, I'll be there encouraging you and writing letters of recommendation."

I blushed at her flattery. "As my grandmother used to say, you are going to give me 'the big head.'"

"No, I'm serious. You were fantastic. This was a hard lesson to teach, but your personal stories made it come to life."

"You don't need to worry about me taking your job," I said. "Do you know how long I spent preparing for this one class? I don't know how you do it day after day."

"You get quicker with practice. To say thank you, can I buy you lunch? Or dinner sometime if you'd prefer?"

"You are too kind. Really, it was my pleasure to try something new. How about if we just find a time for dinner just for fun? You don't owe me a thing."

"It's a plan!" Gail said. "If this wasn't too awful of an experience, would you be willing to come back again sometime?"

"Why don't you ask your students first? If they were bored, I'd hate to repeat it."

"Trust me, if they were bored, they wouldn't have asked questions or joined the conversation. I will ask them what they took away, though. That'll be a good review."

Since it was still quite a while before lunch, I decided to head home. I would come back another time to visit with Mr. Carroll. Driving back to the farm, I thought about my morning and was surprised at how happy I felt. Although I wasn't proficient at self-reflection yet, I believed there were several reasons for my happiness. First, it truly was a blessing to give back. If I had sparked an interest in a young person in the same room where my love of government and law had been kindled, that would be a wonderful blessing. Second, it was also incredibly exciting to have tried something I had never done before—teaching a group of high school students.

I also realized I was happy because of the changes that had occurred within me since I'd come home. I was not the same person who had arrived here just a few short weeks previously. I relived the awakening I'd had at the funeral and thought about all my grandmother's lessons. It really had been an awakening. I felt more alive than I had for a long time. My life in the city had been comfortable, and I had felt safe in my routine. But I was always so busy that I never had time to reflect, grow as a person, or think about whether I was happy. My life was almost womb-like. Safe, comfortable, constrained, and cozy.

Here, I was free, open, and able to breathe deeply and inhale nature, and I had time to think and pray. There was time to think about the past, but more importantly, there was time to think about today. In a way, I felt newly alive. I was free to explore—not just the land and the community I barely knew anymore, but more importantly, my own soul.

I thought again about the lessons from my grandmother. It was strange but comforting that she knew me so well. I hadn't realized it until she pointed it out, but I *had* spent years hiding and running—running from my past toward some nebulous achievement. I had spent most of my teen years and adult life hiding from God and my true self, and trying to prove to myself and the world that I was capable.

When I was in high school, I thought a powerful career would be a way to leave the dust of the farm and my problems behind. Since then, I'd never looked back, and I had never given my career choice a second thought. Now, I was questioning everything.

Ordinarily, such questioning would bring with it a sense of terror, but instead, I now viewed it as an exciting adventure.

No, I was not the same person. I was happy. My smile continued the entire trip back to the farmhouse.

But my smile faded when I arrived home. I found a note from my aunt telling me that my business partner had called and that it was imperative that I return his call. I knew what he wanted, but I had no answer for him.

"Hi, Dave. It's Lydia. I understand you called."

"Yeah, I did!" he said. "What's going on?"

"What do you mean?"

"You know what I mean." His voice rose as his anger increased. "What's going on with you? When are you coming back?"

"I don't know."

"You don't know what?" he yelled.

I was determined not to allow his anger to influence me. I calmly replied, "I don't know when I'm returning."

He screamed so loudly that I pulled the phone away from my ear. "Lydia, I demand that you make some decisions. And if you don't, then I will make them for you! Make a decision about when you are returning, or I will take over your share of the business." And then he hung up.

I sat silently with the phone in my hands. In the past, both Dave's anger and his threat would have had some impact on me. I never would have allowed a hostile takeover of my portion of the business. And yet, now, I simply sat there, staring at the phone. I had no answer for when I would return. Something kept calling me to stay where I was. How could I explain to him what I didn't understand myself? All I knew was that I had no desire to return to my previous life.

Chapter 20

FROM YEARS OF HABIT, Aunt Lu always jumped to answer the phone. Grandmother had simply not been able to reach the phone quickly, so Aunt Lu had long been the one to answer. In my time at the farmhouse, I had quickly fallen into the habit of letting her answer. But on the fourth ring today, however, I realized she wasn't in the house. I hurried to answer it and was delighted to hear Gail's voice when I picked up the phone.

"I'd love to fulfill my obligation to treat you to dinner," Gail said.

"I had such a wonderful time yesterday meeting and talking to your students that I feel as though I should treat you," I said.

"I'm glad to hear you enjoyed it, Lydia, but I want to do this for you."

"That's so sweet of you. My schedule is wide open, so you name the time," I told her.

"Would this Saturday evening work for you? Even though I love my job, by Friday evening, I'm tired. Saturday would give me some time to rest and tackle some household duties too."

"Saturday evening is perfect. Now, the harder question. Where should we go?"

"I know it's a bit of a drive, but there is a lovely restaurant

I dearly love. It's about thirty miles from here, and I would be willing to drive."

"That sounds great. And the drive will give us time to chat."

"Wonderful! I will make the reservation, and I will pick you up at five thirty."

Gail picked me up as promised, and we spent the trip talking about her students and their reaction to my talk. As she had predicted, the kids greatly enjoyed the presentation, and some of them were still talking about it.

The restaurant Gail picked was locally owned restaurant and claimed they served the best steaks in the area. I'd never been there, so I was excited to see if the steaks lived up to their claim.

After we ordered, I told Gail that I had never known anyone who loved what they did as much as she did.

"Really?" Gail said, her eyes wide with surprise. "Oh, Lydia, that's sad."

"Sad but true."

"Are you telling me that you don't really love what you do?" Gail asked.

"I'm not sure what I even do anymore. I have no desire to go back, and I can't explain why." I sighed and fidgeted in my seat.

"You seem a little upset about that," Gail said. "Do you want to talk about it?"

"I'm not sure. I think I'm simply confused. For as long as I can remember, I wanted to be a lawyer. Then I fell into the political world, and it was exhilarating. Working with the people you saw in the news was heady and intoxicating. Even though there was pressure, I thought I would be there forever." I looked away.

"So, what's changed?"

"Being back here. For some reason, I just can't leave. I had a huge argument with my business partner. He called demanding to know when I was returning. When I told him I had no return date in mind, he blew up. He told me that if I didn't tell him exactly when I was coming back, he was taking over the business. But even that had no impact on me. I just can't seem to move. It's like I'm glued to this place."

"Have you considered that God is telling you that you need to stay here?"

"Recently, yes, that has crossed my mind. I've been thinking about my purpose in life and about my passions. But if I stay, what is there here for me?"

"Are you serious? There's always a need for lawyers, even in a small town. No, the real power, as you say, may not be here, but what about helping someone honestly in need?"

I couldn't respond. I didn't know what to say, so I just sat there, looking off into space.

"Or maybe you're just supposed to stay for a while and really clear things up for yourself." Gail paused for a moment. Then, quietly, she asked, "May I speak frankly with you?"

"Somehow, I suspect you will even if I say no," I joked.

"Yeah, you're probably right. Here it goes. What's important to you? You mentioned that it was intoxicating, working where the power was. Is that important to you? Truly important? Here's how I view it—money and power are not what's important. You talked about purpose. I don't think God gives a hoot about either money or power. I mean, think about this. He sent His son to be our savior. Did He send Him as a conquering military leader or as a governmental ruler? No, He sent Him as the son of a carpenter.

Do you see the importance in that? He sends the insignificant to do impossible things. Most of the things we spend our lives pursuing don't mean anything to God.

"I think what's crucial is to live authentically, or maybe it would be better to say that we should live as God designed us— pursuing our divine purpose. I believe we are all on a unique path, and following that path as God intended is what we are designed to do. What talents and gifts did God give you? How does He want you to use them? How should you live using those gifts in the life that God designed for you? I don't think you'll truly be happy until you are authentically following that God-designed path. That may mean a drastically different life for you, but you'll need to talk to God about that.

"And, while I'm on a roll, I will admit that since I first met you, I've suspected you weren't genuinely happy. I may be wrong, but that's what I sensed." She paused to take a breath. "I've gone on and on! If I'm way off base on any of this, I apologize. But I just felt I needed to say all of that."

In the past, I would've been offended by Gail's forward comments, but I surprised myself when I realized I wasn't upset at all. Instead, I decided to share a little about the book that Grandmother had left me. I explained that much of what Gail had said echoed many of the things Grandmother had said in her lessons to me. Gail said she had admired Grandmother's wisdom and faith. The conversation then moved to the subject of prayer, and I shared that I had finally begun to pray.

At that, Gail smiled. "You're on the right path, my friend. To know God's will, we must ask and then listen. Prayer is the way to do that."

I told Gail I would think about all that she'd said. I would pray about God's purpose for my life and where and how that would take place.

Although I didn't tell Gail about them, I knew I still had demons from my past that I needed to face. Soul-searching had occupied much of my time since I had come home, and I was about to do more. *This is hard work*, I thought.

Once I had greeted Aunt Lu, I excused myself and headed upstairs. I wondered if everyone thought about things the way Gail did. Was I the only one who was shallow and just lived day-to-day? I settled down on the bed in my room and flipped through the TV channels, finally settling on something to watch, but it didn't hold my attention. The more I thought about my life, the more I realized I must not have been alone in how I lived. The show was complete drivel, and I turned it off.

I stood and looked in the mirror, studying my reflection. I smiled as I realized that I rather liked the person I was becoming. I wondered if Grandmother was smiling as well.

Chapter 21

EVEN THOUGH THE MEMBERSHIP of my church was small, the women of the congregation hosted an amazing garage sale. It drew people from the entire county. The women considered it a multipurpose event: a mission project and a fellowship gathering as well. The money they raised went to different charities, and the items people donated were priced to sell. The low prices meant that many who were hurting financially could afford to buy clothes for their growing children. Shoppers felt good in knowing that the money they were spending went to people even less fortunate than themselves. The women of the church knew that many of these families would struggle to afford clothes any other way.

Since I was still in town when the event was scheduled to take place, I offered to help. I hadn't volunteered for it since I was in high school. In a way, it was surprising that they still held the sale. It seemed that so many traditions in small communities had to stop because there weren't enough volunteers. Fortunately, this one had continued.

I asked one of the organizers what I could do to be of service and was asked if I would be willing to pick up the many items that Mrs. Dalton had to donate.

Mrs. Dalton and my grandmother had been the best of friends. When I was young, I had often wondered how these two women could spend hours on the phone. What could be new for them to talk about? Now, I realized, they had just talked about life. Rural life at that time could be isolating, and simply talking to a friend was entertainment. As a child, I had loved visiting her home. There was always something yummy to eat, and she always seemed genuinely pleased to see me.

I pulled into the familiar driveway that led up to Mrs. Dalton's home. The house somehow looked like an old friend. After all these years, it was still the same unique shade of green. At the sound of tires on the gravel, Mrs. Dalton came out of the barn to see who had arrived. I jumped out of the car to greet the eighty-something-year-old woman. She wasn't that much younger than Grandmother, and yet, here she was, out in the barn doing chores.

"How are you this morning, Mrs. Dalton?" I asked as she approached.

"Well, Lydia, it is so good to see you! I'm doing just fine. I had to feed the cattle and milk that old dairy cow of mine. How are you?"

"I'm doing great. Are you really still milking your own cows?" After I blurted that out, I realized how disrespectful it sounded. Mrs. Dalton was certainly able to do her own chores, and she had made it known that she would until the day she died.

I was relieved when she laughed and said, "I'm not dead yet."

"I'm so sorry. I didn't mean any disrespect."

"Yes, I know, dear. You just aren't used to seeing people do real work, are you?" she said with a wink.

Now it was my turn to laugh. Not only was she still milking cows, but she was obviously still mentally alert enough to make jokes about my work environment.

"What can I do for you this morning?" Mrs. Dalton asked.

"I understand you have some donations for the church garage sale."

"Yes, I do. Did you come to take those for me? That would be wonderful. I still have work to get done around here, so that would be a real help to me. Let's go up to the house and gather it all."

She led the way. When we reached the porch door, I was delighted to hear the squeak of the hinges. I loved a squeaky door on an old house. I thought it added character.

"Before we get to that stuff, let's have a cup of coffee."

"I'd love a cup."

"I also made a coffee cake this morning. Would you like a piece?"

"Are you having a piece?" I asked.

"Of course I am. I've worked up an appetite."

"I haven't done a bit of work this morning, Mrs. Dalton," I joked. "Is it still okay if I have some?"

"An honest politician, admitting you haven't done a lick of work. For that reason alone, you deserve some."

I smiled. "Now, you know I'm not a politician. I just worked with them."

"Close enough. And did my ears hear correctly? You just said *worked*, past tense."

"Nothing gets by you, does it?"

"I may be old, but I'm still quick."

"Yes, you are."

"Well, *was* that the past tense?"

"And you're tenacious . . . you just keep with it, don't you?"

"That's how I keep going. Now, what's the answer?"

I sat down at the kitchen table with my steaming mug of

coffee. Mrs. Dalton cut two pieces of coffee cake and brought them to the table as she waited patiently for my answer.

"I'm not sure. My business partner is not pleased that I haven't returned yet."

"I suspect not. You've never been gone for this long, and he's confused. The real question is, why haven't you gone back?"

"I just can't make myself go. It's like I'm glued here for some reason. Of course, I can't explain it to anyone else because I don't completely understand it myself. I have finally realized that I've spent my life running and hiding, and now—well, I don't want to run anymore. I'm confused about my whole purpose in life. I just know that when I think about going back, I feel almost panicked about it, and I must confess that I feel incredibly sad about leaving this place."

"There's nothing to explain," Mrs. Dalton told me. "You've got the land in your blood."

"What?"

"You have the farm life in your blood. Now that you've slowed down long enough to realize it, your soul is telling you that you are home."

"Are you talking like Scarlet O'Hara or something? That's such a cliché."

"Clichés often have a bit of truth in them. That's why they came to be. You can scoff at me if you wish, but then explain yourself. Why don't you want to go back to a life that you worked for as hard as you could since you graduated high school? You breezed through college and law school. You went to work for these politicians and about worked yourself to death, according to your grandmother. Never took a vacation. Worked twelve to sixteen hours a day. Now, suddenly, you don't want to go back to the life you almost killed yourself for. You want to stay here, in this boring farm community. What could be the reason for that? I stand by what I said. You've got the farm in your soul."

I didn't know how to respond. The coffee cake almost stuck in my throat. *Scarlet O'Hara longing for Tara?* Was I really feeling that this was where I permanently belonged? Was I meant to be here long-term? Mrs. Dalton was right. I'd worked extremely hard to run from this place, from this life, and from everything it represented. Now, I couldn't bring myself to leave.

Perhaps there was some truth to what Mrs. Dalton said about the land being in my blood, but I had a sense that coming home meant something a bit different and deeper for me. I just couldn't determine what that meant yet.

Somehow, I managed to finish my food and my coffee. Mrs. Dalton helped me load the donations into the car, and I was quiet as we packed everything in the trunk. I'm certain she could tell she'd hit a nerve because I was so quiet. I was thinking. There were no answers yet, but I was definitely thinking.

When I reached the church, several people helped me unload the donations. The preparations for the sale went on for a week. There was organizing and sorting, and, of course, things that needed to be priced. Finally, the day of the sale arrived. It was a tradition for the pastor to pray and say a few words about the volunteers' meaningful work before the sale began. This time, he also asked me to share a song.

"Thank you, but I don't do solos," I told him.

"Now, Lydia, God gave you a beautiful voice that he meant for you to share."

I thought about arguing, but after working so hard over the course of the week, I just didn't have the energy. I reluctantly agreed, and then I hurried to find Margaret.

"Do you know the song 'God on the Mountain'?" I asked when I finally found her.

"Oh, yes, I know that song," Margaret said.

"Would you play and sing that with me?"

"I'd be honored."

The crowd was beginning to form outside the church doors, and inside, the pastor gathered all the workers together. "This year, I'm going to say a short prayer, and then I've asked Lydia to sing for us."

The pastor thanked God for the workers and asked for a blessing on all who entered the church that day. After he said amen, he nodded at me.

Margaret and I walked to the piano.

"I've asked Margaret to help me today. I hope you like this song as much as I do. I find the lyrics 'for the God on the mountain is still God in the valley' very meaningful and powerful."

Even though Margaret and I had never practiced that song, I thought we did a nice job. Reverend Peters had a big smile on his face when we finished. "Praise God," he said. "What a glorious way to kick off our sale. Some of the folks coming here today have been in the valley for a long time. Through our actions and our kind words, let's show them that the God on the mountain is indeed still God in the valley."

And with those words, a wonderful day began. The shoppers found many bargains for their families. The workers raised money for mission work. And there was much fellowship and celebration among friends.

Chapter 22

I HAD NUMEROUS PLANS for work that needed to be done outside the farmhouse, but the weather hadn't cooperated, and my plans had to be set aside. It had stormed and rained for hours, and I was irritated. I was not accustomed to having my plans fall through. As I drank my coffee and fumed, a familiar truck pulled in the drive.

Sam jumped out of his truck and came running up the steps as I opened the door.

"Hi, Sam," I said. "Why in the world are you out in this mess?"

"It's just a little rain," Sam said, brushing the water off his jacket sleeves.

"It's more like a hurricane or something," I grumbled.

Sam frowned. "Is there something wrong, Lydia?"

"I had all these plans for today, but the weather isn't cooperating." Suddenly, I realized how angry I sounded. I sighed. "I'm sorry. Did you need something?"

"I thought today would be a good day for me to give you an update on things. Good use of time, you know."

"Of course. Come on in and have a cup of coffee."

We sat down at the kitchen table and went over several details concerning the farm. We also discussed the plan for the next few weeks. Then Sam gave me an update on a new insurance plan he was investigating. He wanted my opinion on whether we should invest in it. I was still distracted and stared out the window, ignoring the question.

"Seriously, I need to know what you think," Sam said.

I blinked and looked at him. "About what?"

"Have you listened to anything I've said? About the insurance."

"Oh, yes. Really, Sam, whatever you think."

He frowned at me again. "I'm not sure what's going on with you today. I need to be sure you are willing to do this."

I sighed again. "I'm sorry. But seriously, if you think it's a good idea, then we should do it."

"Fine. Now, forgive me for asking again, but what's wrong with you?"

"It's just this weather. I'm irritated."

"Lydia, listen to me. Some days are rainy, but we need the rain for the crops to grow and you need to have flexible plans. The weather is supposed to clear tonight. Plan to work outside tomorrow. Be a little flexible."

"I just hate all this rain."

Sam looked me in the eye. "You know, it's not like every day is stormy. You have one now and then. Like I said, it helps the crops grow, and it helps us appreciate the sunny days. Just because it rains one day doesn't mean it rains every day."

"That sounded a little like a life philosophy," I said with perhaps too much astonishment in my voice.

"Well, maybe it was." He smiled at me.

"I didn't know you were such a deep thinker."

"There's a lot you don't know about me, Lydia. Spending hours and hours on a tractor gives you time to think. Enjoy the rain today and do something inside that needs to be done. Tomorrow, you can return to your schedule." He pushed back his chair and stood. "Oh, one other thing—you need to realize that God's in charge of the plan, not us."

With that, he left. I sat and thought about our visit, and I realized I'd been rude not to give him my full attention. He wanted and needed my opinion. I also thought about what he had said. *Just because it rains one day doesn't mean it rains every day.* That was a lot of philosophy in a few words. I realized you could often say more with a few words, which was an interesting thought for a lawyer. His deep thoughts had caught me off guard. And I kept thinking about his comment that there was a lot I didn't know about him. Was that just a statement, or was it an invitation to learn more?

I poured myself another cup of coffee.

Chapter 23

TWO WEEKS AFTER MY PRESENTATION to Gail's class, she invited me back. She told me that my attendance was a reward for her students successfully completing their government section. Many of the students had asked more questions as they worked through the unit, and Gail thought my presence would be a reward and a way to authentically answer their questions. I was flattered that she invited me back. When the class period was over and all their questions had been answered, I went to the school cafeteria. I took my lunch tray with what I deemed some questionable-looking food to the teacher's lounge. The teachers all greeted me warmly. Gail had told them what a fabulous job I had done the last time I'd visited.

I sat next to Mr. Carroll. He saw me studying my food and laughed heartily. "Lu has spoiled you with all that home cooking," he teased.

I agreed. When I had lived on my own, I ate out a great deal, but many of my meals were either some type of power bar or a frozen meal. This was no different, but I had become accustomed to my aunt's wonderful meals.

Mr. Carroll asked how I was doing, and I took some time to answer.

"Well, if I'm going to be completely honest, it's been a difficult and confusing time. Every time I turn around, I feel that I'm being faced with something new to think about."

"That sounds exciting!"

"I suppose that's one way to look at it."

"Let's finish up and go talk in my classroom. I have the pleasure of a free period after lunch."

"That would be nice."

After we ate, we walked to Mr. Carroll's classroom.

"So, tell me about this confusion," Mr. Carroll said.

"It seems that since I've been back, I've been inundated with dilemmas and confusion. Something inside of me doesn't want to leave, but I've spent a lifetime building a life that isn't here. Intellectually, it seems foolish to even think about leaving that."

"But what does your gut tell you, hmm? What does your soul tell you?"

"I don't know. I'm not sure I'd even recognize my soul saying something."

"Ahh, that is because you have gone through life living from your head. Maybe your soul is crying out to be heard. Perhaps the something inside of you that doesn't want to leave is your soul, and it is trying to get your attention. Answer this and answer it quickly—what awaits you if you return?"

"My work."

"Work. You didn't even say it enthusiastically. You said it like it was drudgery."

"It's long hours, but it's important. I work with some of the most powerful people in the country."

"Powerful in what way?"

"What do you mean? They write laws and set policies that impact all of us."

"And is that really important to you? Working with these people? Does it bring you joy and satisfaction, or are you out to prove that you can handle playing with the big boys and that you are worthy and are their equal? Or maybe that you're able to stand up to them and even beat them?

"I'm challenging you to look into your very being to see who you were meant to be. Stop trying to prove yourself worthy to the rest of us and prove it to yourself. Don't try to jump on the path you think you should be on or the one you think is most impressive to others. Get on the path you were meant to be on. As soon as you graduated, it was as if you moved as far as you could from here, and I think maybe even from yourself. I'm challenging you to ask yourself why you did that and to think about what you should be doing now. It sounds like something deep within you is begging you to think deeper and that you are being challenged to think about the who and the whys in life."

I sat stunned. Tears boiled up in my eyes, but this time I was able to keep them from falling.

"I know that's a lot to think about," Mr. Carroll said gently, "but I think it needed to be said. I honestly feel that your time here at home has prepared you to think about these things. One more thought: You have many gifts. Do you think you can use those only in your current career?"

"I guess not."

"Of course not. It is possible that you are being called to use those gifts in a different way?"

"I don't know," I told him. "I wish someone would tell me what to do."

"No, you don't. You'd never listen."

I smiled and nodded. "I guess you're right."

"You just have some more thinking to do. But don't limit yourself in your decisions. Be creative. And there's something else I've wanted to talk to you about."

"I don't think I can handle anything else."

"Oh, yes you can. You're one tough lady," he said. "I want you to think about how much you enjoyed writing when you were in high school and remember what a good writer you were."

"What?"

"You were an excellent writer."

"But I haven't written anything other than documents for work in years."

"That is because you've been living from your head. When you were my student and I forced you to think from your heart, your writing was quite good. It's just one more thing to explore. It's a gift that I don't think you've ever considered."

"My head is going to explode if I have one more thing to explore."

"Don't use your head for this," he said. "At least, not only your head. Let your heart speak to you. I think the true answer might be found there. You need to feel from your heart and soul and then let your head interpret and process the information. I also feel that you might have some sort of healing to do, and for many people, writing can be a wonderful way to sort through it all."

"Do I just wear everything on my sleeve for the world to see?" I asked.

The corners of his mouth twitched upward, and his eyes twinkled. "Quite the opposite. I think you have your feelings frozen inside of you somewhere, and they need to thaw. Usually, that's caused by a hurt that has been covered up. You need to allow yourself to heal from whatever those wounds are, or you are never truly going to live."

"Maybe I'll try some writing. Did you know that Grandmother wrote too? Actually, she kept a journal of sorts."

"I didn't know, but I'm not surprised. Your grandmother was a deep thinker. I noticed, especially later in her life, that she relied on her faith for guidance. Keeping a journal can be helpful as you are exploring your faith and your walk. Does that make sense?"

"I guess so," I said. "As you discover things that you believe, you can look back at past thoughts and see how you have grown."

"Exactly. You can also write down prayers and concerns and see how God answers those."

The bell rang to signal the end of the period.

I stood from my chair. "I guess that's my signal that I need to go. Thank you so much for your time, Mr. Carroll. I really appreciate it."

"I hope I didn't overwhelm you today, Lydia."

"No, not at all. But it does seem like I've been bombarded with these kinds of talks since I've been home."

Mr. Carroll smiled. As I walked out the door, he called to me. "I'd be honored to read any of your writings, Lydia."

I smiled and nodded to him as I headed into the crowded hallway. When several students smiled and said hello to me, I was caught off guard. A couple of students even asked when I'd come back to talk to them again.

I said I would talk to their teacher, but that I really didn't know. They told me they hoped it would be soon, and I couldn't help but smile.

Chapter 24

WHEN I AWOKE THE NEXT MORNING, I realized that I wanted to learn about farming. Really learn. Learn everything there was to know. This was now my farm, but I understood little about the day-to-day operations. When we talked before, Sam had explained some of the basics of how the farm operated. He had told me what I needed to know to make some decisions, but now, I wanted to know everything.

I couldn't reach Sam by phone, so I decided to drive to the various fields to look for him. It took me about thirty minutes to find him. He was a little surprised and concerned when he saw me and thought something must be wrong. I sheepishly told him my desire to learn more about the farm operations. He stood there for a minute, seemingly not quite sure how to react, and then finally asked if everything had been working out to my satisfaction.

"Oh, yes, everything is fine," I said. "It's just that, well, it seems that I should truly know how this place runs. I've always been a take-charge person, and I'd just like to know what is going on. That way, if you ask my advice on something again, we might actually be able to discuss it." I paused and then added, "Instead of me pretending that I understand what you're saying."

Sam studied me for a minute and then burst out laughing. "You mean, when we were discussing all that stuff before and I was asking you your opinion, you really had no idea what I was talking about?"

"Well, truthfully? No. I just trusted your decision."

He laughed even harder. "I thought to myself later that you sure seemed to know what I was talking about, and I was a little surprised. But you were always so smart, I thought you had picked it up somewhere."

He watched me for another minute. "Are you thinking that you might stay?"

"Would it bother you if I did?"

"Of course not. Why would you even ask that?"

"I don't want to be in your way, Sam. You've done such a good job for my grandmother. I'm not asking you to teach me because I'm not happy with your work."

"Whoa, slow down. I just meant that I know it would be a big decision for you. You've been a city girl for so long, I just didn't know if you could stand our slower way of life." He leaned against the truck and smiled at me.

"To be honest," I said, "since I've been here, I've realized that I didn't really have a life there. I worked and slept, but I did nothing else. Is that living? It no longer feels real or authentic to me. It all seems rather . . . plastic."

His smile faded, and he gave me a serious look. "That may be the first honest, authentic thing I've ever heard you say."

I blushed. This farmer could see people for who they really were, and I was certain that he was looking directly into my soul. I blinked back tears, wondering whether he could see my deep wounds and lifelong anguish.

I changed the subject quickly. "Well, sir, are you willing to take on a student?"

"I'd be pleased to teach you about your farm."

With that, the tutoring began. We spent the entire day together. As we maneuvered through the fields, he explained what he was doing. At one point, he even insisted that I drive the tractor. I argued, but he insisted that to really learn, I needed to experience. I think Sam was surprised at how determined and focused I was. Perhaps he didn't realize that those were the skills I needed in my career: extreme determination and complete laser focus.

Throughout the day, I noticed Sam watching me. I wondered again if he could see the old wounds I carried or whether he could tell that I was slowly healing. Or perhaps he was simply concerned about whether I could handle the expensive farm equipment. I wasn't sure what he was thinking, but I finally quit worrying about it because I needed to concentrate on what I was doing.

When the day's lesson was over, I went home and dropped into a chair. I was more physically exhausted than I could ever remember being. Wow! Farming was hard physical work, even with all the modern assistance of tractors and other equipment.

Aunt Lu just shook her head at me. "You know, Lydia, you don't have to learn the whole operation in one day."

"Sam seemed willing to teach me today, so I thought I should take advantage of that."

"I just hope you can move tomorrow."

I simply nodded. After I had eaten some dinner, I went upstairs with the intention of sitting in Grandmother's room and looking through a few more things. But when I reached the top of the stairs, I realized I was too tired. I dropped onto my bed and was asleep almost as soon as my head touched the pillow.

Chapter 25

THE NEXT MORNING, after I had read the newspaper and finished a second cup of coffee, I headed out to the garden. On my way to pick strawberries, I noticed some flowers that needed their dead blooms trimmed back. After I made it through the first bed, I sat back and looked at my work. My grandmother's choice of flowers and the variety in the colors were simply magnificent. I smiled at the realization that God's crayon box must be huge to handle all this beauty.

I also realized how much I enjoyed caring for these flowers. My hands were filthy and my nails were a mess, but I thought it was beautiful. This realization that I enjoyed working with my hands caught me completely by surprise. When I was a child, I had absolutely dreaded this sort of work. I'd hated every minute of it. Now, it was a joy! It didn't seem like work at all. Simply being outside was wonderful. The fresh air allowed me to breathe deeper than I had ever been able to in the city. It was as if I needed to inhale as much nature as I could.

I looked skyward. The clouds were beautiful. There were just a few puffy, pure-white clouds. When was the last time that I had even noticed clouds? I usually walked quickly, looking at the ground so I wouldn't trip over something or someone as I was talking on my cell phone. What had all those conversations been about, anyway? Had I really contributed to the general good? Or was I just serving people who wanted to enrich themselves and not humanity as a whole?

These thoughts had never occurred to me before. I was questioning the purpose of my entire adult working life. I sat on the ground and continued to look up to the sky. *God, help me. My life seems to be at a potential turning point. Do I continue my current path or choose a completely unknown road?* I had never prayed like this before. Somehow, I knew this was *the* most important thing I could be doing. I waited for an answer, expecting God to simply point out the path. Maybe even use a cloud as an arrow. But I quickly realized that I might not receive answers immediately.

As I sat and gazed at my surroundings, I recognized that life on this farm provided me with much more time to think. The quiet here allowed me to better hear God talking to me. *Ah*, I realized, *that's what Grandmother was saying in her lesson about prayer. The key is that you must be able to hear God's answer. Most of the world has so much noise and so many distractions that people cannot quiet themselves to hear God. That's what is so refreshing about life on this glorious farm.*

I paused and waited, but there were no answers today. Just peace.

After I finished my work outside, I soon found myself drawn to my grandmother's room once again, and more specifically, to the journal. I opened the book to another lesson. The title had frightened me, so I had not yet read it. It was called "Stop Running."

My dear granddaughter,

It has been difficult for me to find the words for this lesson. It has been on my heart for a long time, but the right words simply would not come. I have prayed about it for quite some time. I hope that the words now given to me are from God. This is a lesson that I think you need to hear from Him and not just from me. I also have a little more strength today, so I'm going to preach a bit.

You must stop running from your past. Your past has not been pleasant—I know this. But there are many people who have had very unpleasant pasts, and they have learned to move forward. On the surface, most people think that you have moved on as well. I, however, see such pain in your soul. I do not know the exact cause of it, but I do know this: you have hidden yourself from God. You have been running as far from home as you can. As I said before, I do not know if it is from this place or from your family—or simply from your past—but I do feel strongly that the result is you have been running from your true self as well as from God. Something that happened has hurt you to your core. By running from it, you have also decided that you need to hide yourself from God.

You must stop running. Running solves nothing. You must face this pain and process it. You must stop running from God and turn to Him. Remember what I wrote before—God loves us no matter what. We think that we must be perfect to deserve His love and forgiveness, but this is a lie. It is God's grace that gives us love and forgiveness. We have all sinned, and God forgives all of us. We do not earn it. We do not deserve it. God willingly and lovingly gives us His love and forgiveness. If God loves us and forgives us, and He does, then we should drop to our knees and praise Him for His grace. And at that same moment, we need to accept our own forgiveness. I know that last part is difficult, but it is crucial. To truly live God's redemption, you must also forgive yourself.

Lydia, I don't know what has caused your pain. But this I know: There is no sin that God will not forgive if we ask. There is no moment beyond God's desire and capacity for redemption. Hear that again. There is no moment beyond God's desire and capacity for redemption! Praise God! There is redemption for all! Yes, Lydia, that redemption is for you as well! Ask Him. You must ask God, and He will forgive. And then you need to forgive yourself, even if it takes time.

I also wonder if perhaps the running comes from shame. Constantly living in shame can feel like living in a cave. It is isolating, dark, cold, and depressing. It is a deep, dark, foreboding place. The foundation of shame is the belief that you have disappointed yourself and, more importantly, disappointed God. But do you know what is even worse than living in constant shame? It is not realizing or accepting that there is redemption. And what did I just say? There is no moment or any sin that is beyond God's desire and capacity for redemption. God and His redemption are the anecdote for shame!

Please hear this, Lydia: you need to stop running so you can find what you are truly seeking. Stop running and open your heart to God. My dear one, you must find redemption from your past to truly embrace your future. You must stop running so that you can recover what you have lost. I hope that you will pray about this.

Once you stop running from God and run to Him, all your sins—and I mean all—will be forgiven. Do you remember one of my favorite songs, "It is Well with My Soul"? It says, "My sin, not in part, but the whole is nailed to the cross, and I bear it no more. Praise the Lord!" The whole, Lydia, the whole of my sin will be forgiven. Isn't that something to celebrate?

Please hear this as well. I know that your grandfather and I were your grandparents and not your parents, but I don't think we could have loved you more. Yes, we may have shown our love in an old-fashioned way, but search your heart to know that we did love you. You are and always have been surrounded by people who love you. However, I believe you must forgive yourself and love yourself before you can truly realize how loved you are.

And I must add this as well: after you invite God into your life, you will never be the same. It will be so very rich—in ways that many people never understand. It will be rich in peace and in grace. It is such a joyous and amazing thing to follow God's path for you. Choose that path, Lydia, and you will be truly—not superficially, but truly—blessed.

That hit hard, but the next lesson appeared to be just as difficult to read. Even though I was tired, something drew me to continue reading. This one was entitled, "Shame."

I touched on this subject before, but I want to come back to it. I have read and put a great deal of thinking and prayer into this subject. I encourage you to do the same, Lydia. I encourage you to do this because I truly wonder if shame is at the core of your unhappiness.

Shame comes from falling short. Not measuring up. I'm wondering if this is part of the reason why you work so hard. You are trying to measure up to something. Shame comes from judgment, and it can be external or internal judgment. Thus, the constant drive to prove something—to measure up.

In my reading, I have discovered that when a person experiences extreme shame, the ego will do anything to protect itself, and the soul longs to be healed because it is wounded. The ego will build defenses or fortifications to help protect the wounded soul.

Lydia, do you see why I think this sounds like you? You have spent years building mighty walls to defend yourself, but in truth, that makes everything worse. The soul desperately wants and needs to commune with God, but since it is wounded, it is difficult to do so. In trying to protect the soul, the ego hides the soul from God and prevents true healing.

In my mind, I can see you hiding in a corner with your face buried in your knees, trying to look as small as possible. Without accepting God's love, you will remain in that corner. When the soul is wounded, all the pieces are still present. Even if the soul is shattered, the pieces are still there, and it can still be healed.

You could ignore the hurt or pretend it is not so bad.

But if you do that, then healing will not occur. You need to reach out, and then God will reach back. You must take the first step.

Take that first step, Lydia. God is waiting. You may believe that healing and redemption cannot happen, but they can. All the pieces are there, and they can be healed. The pieces may not be quite the same as before, but they can be healed. I pray that you have the courage to take the first step. I believe you do! Redemption and healing can be yours.

Love and prayers,
Grandmother

I could not stop reading. I plunged into the next lesson, though silent tears poured down my face. The next title was "Anger and Trust."

My dear Lydia,

I want to speak to you today about a topic I should have addressed when you were much younger: anger.

I see an immense anger in you. Most of the world never sees this part of you. To them, you appear calm, never flustered or frustrated. I, however, see an anger boiling just under the surface. I see it in your eyes. I see it in your face when it goes stone-cold and when you are pushing all emotions down. I see it in your desire to work more hours today than you did yesterday. If you don't learn to process your anger, it will continue to come out in the same unhealthy ways, over and over.

157

When you try to ignore the anger, the only solution you have is to repeat the same behavior that seems to sooth it temporarily. Your addiction—yes, that is what I call your workaholic nature—is how you try to survive your pain and brokenness. It might seem odd that I call being a workaholic an addiction, but it is as spiritually and physically harmful as many other addictions. Yes, my child, I see it. And I am acknowledging it even if you don't want to.

Although I don't know with certainty where this anger comes from, I have thoughts about its origin. You are a wounded woman. I've mentioned this in many of these lessons, and I acknowledge that you have been deeply hurt. I surmise that you may feel abandoned and unloved. You seem to have lost hope and faith in everything except your ability to work hard, but I think what you may have lost the most is your faith and trust in God. I sense that you believe God has let you down. That He has not protected you from pain, and you are angry at Him for that.

My dear Lydia, God has never said we would not have pain. God said He would walk with us through our pain. Like a dear friend, God is with us, bringing us comfort in our darkest days. God does not cause the pain. Hear me on this, Lydia: God did not cause your pain. Pain is simply part of our human life.

I urge you to pray about this. Turn to God with your questions of faith and trust. Yes, it may seem odd to turn to the creator whom you have lost trust in to ponder trust, but I believe with all that I am that is what you need to do. Trust God, Lydia. Put your love and trust in Him.

Once you have done that, then you need to deal with your anger in a positive way. That is the only way the anger will dissipate. Ignoring it and trying to shove it down where you cannot see it is not the way. Do not be afraid of it. It is normal to have emotions, but you need to face them. Acknowledge your anger. Write about it. Sing about it. Search for ways to process this powerful emotion and then put that energy to a positive use. If you keep burying it, then the anger will erupt in a negative or nonproductive way.

I must be honest with you that processing your anger will be hard. Anger almost always happens when a guiding or core value has been broken. Everything that you have told yourself about this value and your anger needs to be addressed. The reward for this hard work will be worth it! When you process your anger in a positive way, it will move you toward restoring that broken value. Processing your anger, and really, I must call it recovery, cannot be done alone. You will need a trusted friend or perhaps a professional counselor to help you.

I believe that your anger will begin to subside when you reconcile with God. When you fully accept that you can trust Him, I believe you will be filled with His peace. Then, your anger will be easier to manage. You will be on your way to healing.

One other point about trust. Trust is different than love. We can love God but still want to do things our way and on our own terms. Trust is when we realize that God knows what is best for us. Not our way, but God's way. Trust is when we realize that, not only can God provide what is best, but He will provide what is best. Trust is realizing we were never truly in control anyway, and it is turning over the illusion to the one who is in control. My hope is that you will learn this important lesson earlier than I did. Sometimes it takes us strong-willed women time to learn things.

Pray about this, my dear Lydia: not my will, but Thy will be done.

Grandmother

Once again, I discovered that I had not taken a breath as I read Grandmother's lessons. I was no longer surprised by the tears that rolled down my cheeks. Since I had no tissues, I wiped them on my sleeve. On these subjects, as with so many others, Grandmother was correct. Had I been running? Yes, I had. That would explain why I was always so emotionally exhausted. When it came to the lesson on shame, I didn't think I had the emotional strength to fully face it. Somehow, Grandmother had nailed it. It was hard to admit, but I felt so much shame that I couldn't look in a mirror. The debilitating fear I felt, particularly here, was that others knew about my past or would discover it. When I spoke to people, I wondered if they knew the things I had done as a teenager. I was always afraid they were judging me, but no one could judge me as harshly as I judged myself.

As for my anger, for years, I *had* kept my boiling temper just under the surface. I lived in fear that it would erupt at any moment. Grandmother was also correct when she wrote that she wondered if I had lost my faith and trust. Oh yes, she was correct. I had felt anger at God for years. I was angry because I felt He had not protected me. I blamed God for all my pain—my parents' death, the incident in high school, and everything that followed. Yes, I had spent most of my life blaming God for not protecting me. I was angry because my value of trust was broken, and I blamed God for it.

I was beginning to understand, not just in my head, but in my soul, that trusting God meant knowing God loved me and was always with me. Pain would still happen, but God would be with me in it. He would not abandon me.

Just as with the other lessons, I knew I had work to do. This anger had been with me for a long time. It would take time to process it and to learn how to put that energy to a positive use. That would take work. I also had learned enough already to know it would take time and a great amount of prayer to move from my old ways of trusting only myself to fully trusting God.

My woundedness had led me into the addiction of being a workaholic. Not only did my long work hours distract me so that I didn't have time to face my woundedness, but it allowed me to establish an artificial value that I could control. Although my addiction led me to human success, it did not move me toward repairing my value of trust.

I wept as I realized it would have been safe to be angry in Grandmother's presence. She understood. She knew that the life I was living wasn't in alignment with my values, and she could have helped me process my anger instead of letting it weigh me down all these years. I think Grandmother grieved because I couldn't get my anger out in a positive way. I vowed to honor her by beginning this long journey, starting by admitting that I could and would trust God.

Everything came flashing back in my mind. Even though I didn't want to face it, I knew I had to if I was ever going to move forward. First, the pain from losing my parents. And then the pain from that first incident with the boy at the county park. "Incident"—what a euphemism! I recognized, perhaps for the first time, that the incident was, in fact, date rape. Although some people may have viewed putting myself in that position as a poor choice, it was rape. I don't know if I yelled for him to stop or if my voice remained as paralyzed as my body, but being unable to move or speak during such a traumatic event was *not* consent. I had made it quite clear that I wanted him to stop.

My conduct after the rape were tragic. What I couldn't yet grasp was that my actions were those of a young girl who was trying to make sense of the world. The trust I had put in men had been shattered. By repeatedly putting myself in the same predicament, I was trying, in part, to prove that my value of trust was intact. I so desperately wanted a different answer or result even though I kept acting in the same way. I'd wanted someone to prove that trust and respect were still possible. I suppose this lack of trust in people led me to lose my trust in God as well.

My shame and broken values had caused me to question everything about myself to the point that I'd lost who I was. My pain had caused me to continue to run away from my true self. Perhaps the reason I ran toward a powerful career was because I thought that would allow me to be in control.

Instead, I simply felt the pain of my shame. Grandmother had understood, and she was correct. I had to stop running. I had to find redemption from my past if I wanted a new future.

Chapter 26

I HEARD THE PHONE RING downstairs, and then Aunt Lu called up to me. "You've got a call, Lydia!"

I quickly wiped away my tears and went to answer the phone.

Gail's bubbly voice greeted me, and she asked if I would like to come over and have dinner with her the following night. I was exhausted from Grandmother's lessons, but something made me tell Gail yes. After I hung up, I thought about talking to Gail about the journal. I thought maybe it would be good to bounce some ideas off another person, and I really trusted her wisdom. Grandmother's words, *soul friend*, kept coming to mind.

The next evening, I enjoyed an excellent dinner that Gail prepared, and the conversation was comfortable. As we lingered over dessert and coffee, I asked her about the timing of the invitation.

"Did you have something you wanted to talk about?" I asked my hostess.

"No, why do you ask?" Gail said, frowning. It was obvious that she was confused by my question. "Do we need a reason to enjoy good food and conversation?"

"No, it's just that it was really good timing for me, and I thought it must be . . . a God-thing that you called."

"Well, now I'm intrigued."

I decided to jump right in. "I've been reading more of the lessons that Grandmother wrote for me. Honestly, I've been struggling with some of them. Yesterday, when you called, I had just finished a couple of particularly emotional ones, and I thought it might be nice to talk to someone about them."

Gail leaned forward. "Any lessons from your grandmother would be lessons I would like to learn. You know, I think she had such wisdom. It wasn't boastful. It was a wisdom that came from truly living and observing. I'd love to hear about what she said."

I shared Grandmother's observation that I had been running and that I thought perhaps she was correct. Then, I posed a question to Gail. "How do you know what path you should be on or, perhaps even more bluntly stated, who you truly are when you've spent years running from yourself and from God?"

Gail exhaled slowly. "You just get right to the point, Lydia. No beating around the bush on this one!" She thought for a moment before continuing. "I'm not sure I'm qualified to answer your question, but I believe you're right; it *can* be difficult to discern God's path and message. I have found that, for me, I must pray and pray and pray some more. I will often tell God that I know there's a message waiting for me but that I need help in understanding it. Then, when He answers, I have this calm assurance about the answer I've heard. A sort of knowing that it was a heaven-sent message, if you will.

"At times, the voice has been almost audible. Sometimes I even look around to see who has spoken to me. Other times, it's simply a feeling or an idea that has been placed on my heart. I always feel a sense of peace about it. Sometimes I'll say, 'Yes, but . . .' when I think of reasons why that answer can't be possible. I even have peace about my concerns. Usually, I hear a reassuring voice reminding me that, with God by my side, anything is possible. Sometimes the idea that He has given me is so crazy or so far-fetched that I know it must be from Him. It might be something so crazy that I know I couldn't have thought of it by myself. Does that help at all?"

I nodded. I had experienced some of those feelings myself. I took a deep breath and asked a question I was almost afraid to hear the answer to. "What do you think about me feeling drawn to stay here, leave my career in DC, and go down a completely unknown path?"

Gail looked at me—really looked at me. I felt as though she was trying to look right into my soul.

"Lydia, be honest with me. What happened here when you were a kid? I've had the feeling that you weren't happy here growing up. And for you to ask me that, it makes sense that you're questioning even more than you said."

"It's just—" I couldn't hold it back. My voice broke and tears rolled down my cheeks. I had shed many tears since I'd been back, but I was embarrassed by this lack of control. Gail immediately realized that this show of emotion was important. The remnants of the strong fortress I had built around my soul were crumbling.

She reached out and touched my arm. "I think God is speaking to your soul right now. Do you feel comfortable talking about it?"

"This is totally new for me," I said, sniffling. "I haven't talked about anything like this with anyone before . . . ever."

"Do you want to talk about it?" Gail asked gently.

I was silent for a long time as I weighed the possibilities in my mind. Did I want to talk about something so deeply personal and extremely painful? Finally, I nodded. I took a deep breath and began. "I've been running and hiding for years. I had never viewed my life like that, but when I read Grandmother's words, I knew it was true. Some things happened here when I was younger, and I just wanted to leave my past behind. I wanted to get as far away as I could. Not just away from this place, but from everything. I guess, in a way, the problems continued to follow me even after I left, so instead of just physically running away, I ran away emotionally and spiritually too."

"You ran away from God," Gail said. It wasn't really a question.

"Yes. I realize now that He's the one I've tried to run away from the most." Tears rolled down my cheeks, and I took a deep breath before quietly speaking again. "I've done some things that I question whether He will ever be able to forgive. I'm so ashamed."

Gail gave me a sympathetic look. I could tell from her expression that she realized just how deeply I was hurting.

"Lydia, God loves all of us, and He will forgive *all* our sins if we confess them to Him. He says no sins are too big or too small. Of course He'll forgive you. If you honestly ask Him to, then He will walk with you through the healing." She paused and then said, "Do you believe this?"

I couldn't find my voice, but I nodded.

"You know, Lydia, shame is a very isolating emotion."

I couldn't even find the strength to lift my head, so I stared at the floor.

"What you need most at those times, God and a supportive community of believers, is completely shut off from you. You can feel so ashamed that you don't feel comfortable with others. You have judged yourself right into a frozen cave. God's redemption is the answer and the cure for our shame. Redemption deals fully with our falling short—and we've *all* fallen short. I don't know why you think you can't be forgiven, but you can! Your sins can be forgiven, and your shame can be healed. God can and will deliver you from all your sins. You can bask in God's redemption!"

"A part of me wants to run and to leave this place right now, Gail. As fast and far as I can."

"Why is that?"

I took a deep breath. Should I confide even more in a woman who, in many ways, I barely knew? If I started down this path, I didn't know if I could stop the questions or if I would be able to handle the answers that might come next.

After sitting and looking at my hands folded on my lap, I decided that I really did need to talk to someone about this, so I plunged in. I didn't know what to say or where to begin. My mind was racing with how much to share and how to say it, and I ended up just blurting out, "I'm afraid of Sam."

"What?" Gail asked, her eyes wide in surprise.

I sighed and ran my fingers through my hair in frustration. "That didn't come out right. I don't know what I'm saying or why I'm telling you any of this." I paused for a minute to collect my thoughts. "I'm afraid of my *feelings* for Sam."

Gail sat back in her chair. She had been trying desperately to understand what I was so concerned and upset about, and then a look of understanding came over her.

"Lydia," she said, "are you sure you want to talk about this?"

"I don't know. But I feel like maybe I need to."

"What exactly are you afraid of?"

"I'm afraid that I might be attracted to him."

She gave me a small smile. "Is that a bad thing?"

"Every relationship I've ever had with a man has ended in disaster. I swore I was done with relationships."

"Are you afraid that he might not have the same feelings?"

"No, that's not it."

"Are you more afraid that he might have feelings for you too?"

I simply nodded.

Gail paused for a second, seeming to debate over a question. Finally, she asked, "Lydia, did something happen between you and a man?"

That simple question caused all the years of hurt and shame to come flooding out in a powerful storm of emotion. I sobbed as if I hadn't cried in years and years. My entire body reacted. My soul cried out to God. *God, why did this happen? Why did you forsake me?* What I thought I had trapped and buried exploded out of me in wrenching sobs. Grandmother's words that I needed to find redemption from my past ran through my mind again. Was that truly possible? Could I bask in God's redemption? Could God love me? I'd felt unlovable for so many years. Was it possible for God to love me?

After several long minutes, I looked up at Gail. The story was finally going to be told. "Many years ago, I was raped by my boyfriend. For a long time, I'd felt that it was my fault because I had put myself in the position to allow it to happen. I never should have been there with him or allowed him to . . . I blamed myself because I was unable to physically fight him or make him stop. But recently, I've realized that even though I felt paralyzed by the trauma, I did let him know that I didn't consent. Even if I didn't fight, it was still rape."

I gave myself a minute to find my voice again. "The shame I felt because of what happened led me to make bad choices. I put myself in the same situation over and over, and I continued to let men use me. I guess a part of me hoped that one of them would accept me and the cycle would end. I despised myself and my actions, and a little more of me died with each episode. I thought that even if God could forgive me for putting myself in the position where I was raped, there was no way He would forgive me for my actions afterward. I know I can't forgive myself. This pain, this agony that I carry, I caused so much of it." Once again, uncontrollable sobbing overtook me.

Gail reached out to me and took my hand. "Is this the first time you've shared your story with anyone?"

I nodded.

"I'd like to pray with you, if I may." When I nodded again, she continued. "Heavenly God, please be with my friend, Lydia. She's hurting, and you know that she has been hurting for a long time. Even when she didn't know it, she has been searching for you. Place your healing hand on her right now so that she might know you are here, as you are always right here with us. Though we see only our brokenness, you see our wholeness. Please give her your blessed assurance that she is loved and that all her sins, even those that she thinks are unforgivable, are indeed forgiven. Please comfort her. Bring her peace and guide her as she also has some possible life-changing decisions to make. Most precious God, as always, I thank you for your love of us."

As Gail prayed, it was as if a blanket of comfort and deep-and-knowing peace surrounded me. It felt as if I had drunk a cup of something warm. My entire body tingled. I had once again been blessed by God with a peace so profound that words could not truly describe it. I knew that He had indeed forgiven me for everything. But even more, I knew that He was already walking the road to healing with me. God was telling me He didn't cause my pain, and He had been with me through it all. Even when I didn't realize it, He was waiting for me to reach out. He had not forsaken me.

Gail moved to sit beside me, and we hugged as God began to heal my shattered soul. I knew that He had visited me personally to say, "Yes, my child, even you can be and are completely forgiven."

Several minutes passed before I was finally able to speak again. Then I asked, "Where do I go from here? How do I know that God has forgiven me?" I knew the answer, but I had to ask to confirm it.

"It's not something you know in your head, Lydia. It's something you feel in your soul. God knows when we are truly asking for forgiveness. He knows when we are seeking Him. His love is always there. We just have to accept it."

In my heart, I already knew that God had forgiven me. He had already seen the truth in my soul, and He continued to blanket me with His amazing peace.

"What's next?" I asked.

Gail paused for a moment. "I guess I would say the path forward for me centered on belief, love, and trust. First, I had to believe in God. Then, I had to accept His love for me and love Him in return. And then came trust—trust that He forgave me, trust that He knows what is best for me and can lead me to it, and trust that He can and will heal all my brokenness. Love and trust, Lydia. Those are key."

"This is so much to absorb."

Gail smiled. "Yes, I suppose it is."

"I'm a little overwhelmed."

"Why don't you take one step at a time?" Gail suggested.

She paused for a moment and then added, "May I make a recommendation?"

I nodded.

"I suggest that you work on your relationship with God first. If you focus on that, I think the decisions about what's next for you will become clearer."

Many more minutes passed as we absorbed what had transpired. Finally, I said, "I'm still afraid of Sam."

Gail laughed. "My friend, I hear you. Men are scary. Do you mind if I share my thoughts on this as well?"

"Not at all. That's why I brought it up again."

"For right now, why don't you concentrate on listening to God and discovering the path you are meant to be on? I think, when you do that, you'll know what to think about Sam."

I dug through my purse, looking for a tissue. "I'm so sorry that I unloaded all of this on you."

Gail smiled. "That's what friends do for each other. And just in case you're curious, I think God called you to share this with me. You can't carry around burdens like this alone. You can't continue to live an isolated life. We need a community. I think that's why, after all these years, you knew tonight that you needed to talk about this. You need to talk about things like this with a trusted friend. I hope you know that I think of you that way. And I hope you'll pray about these things too."

"I will," I said. "I've been praying, but I just feel that I—well, now I feel that I have a closer relationship with God."

I looked intently at my friend. "Thank you so much for listening. At first, I guess my shame wanted to keep everything hidden, but now I honestly feel better. Thank you."

"I'm just a friend who's walking through life with you. We are both walking with Jesus on this path."

I choked up a little, and I reached over and hugged her again.

I drove home in silence—no radio, no talking to myself. My mind was a blank canvas. I was physically, emotionally, mentally, and spiritually exhausted. The only thought that came to me was about the peace I was feeling. It was amazing. My soul didn't feel tortured. In fact, it felt as if, after many years, my shattered pieces had been glued back together. They had been there all along, and God put them back together. I could feel His grace shining through my newly repaired soul like a beautiful stained-glass window. Exhaustion, love, joy, and peace—that was what I felt. I went directly to my room, collapsed on the bed, and had the best night's sleep that I could remember in an exceptionally long time.

Chapter 27

WHEN I AWOKE THE NEXT MORNING, I went downstairs and, as with every morning, found Aunt Lu already working in the kitchen. I couldn't help myself. I walked over and gave her a hug.

"Good morning, Aunt Lu. How're you doing this morning?"

"I'm just marvelous, Lydia. How about you?"

Aunt Lu, of course, immediately noticed something different in me. One obvious difference was that I never gave anyone a spontaneous hug. This morning, however, I wanted to hug the entire world.

"I believe I would like to take a cup of coffee outside. Would you mind if I ate breakfast on the porch?"

"Not at all. You go right ahead. God gave us a glorious morning to spend outdoors."

I poured a cup of my aunt's famously strong coffee, added some creamer, and went to sit on the porch. It was indeed a beautiful morning. How many other mornings like this one had I witnessed but never seen? *Enough of that*, I told myself. *There's nothing I can do about the past. I will focus on today!* Then I realized what a wonderful way that was to view my entire past. I couldn't change it, but I could change the present—how I viewed it and how I reacted to it. Another tear rolled down my cheek. *More God washing, I guess.*

I put my coffee cup down and prayed. I told God how thankful I was for His grace and asked for guidance on this new path I was on. Although I wasn't sure where the path was going, I knew it *was* a new path. Suddenly, I realized with assurance that the path was here, on the farm—at least for now. It wasn't back in DC.

I picked up my coffee and started walking toward the orchard. Perhaps I wasn't meant to stay on this farm forever, but for the moment, I heard God telling me that I was meant to be in this place. I still had much to work on and to work through, and this was where I needed to be to resolve those things. The idea both scared and comforted me. It was a strange combination of feelings, and yet I knew it was right. I simply felt it.

There was a peace I felt about this decision, but it was scary. It meant leaving everything behind—my home; what friends, or perhaps they were only acquaintances, I had; and mostly, my life's work. Yes, it was the work I was most scared about leaving. How would I define myself without it? Everyone I knew defined themselves by their careers. The only words they used to describe themselves centered around their jobs. Who would I be without my career, my life's work?

Somehow, I knew there would be a new way to define myself. Soon, my true purpose would be revealed. I felt strongly that I needed to completely step away from the life I had known and into the future. At this moment, I just needed to *be* and not to focus so much on *doing*.

That thought was particularly strange to me, to be and not to do, but I knew that more clarification would eventually come. With a knowing that I couldn't explain, I realized this new path was all about being and not doing. My life's work was just that, work. What I truly needed to focus on was who I was meant to be. Since I had spent most of my life running and trying to prove something, I had never thought about who I was meant to be.

For most of my life, I had hidden behind *what* I was because I was too afraid to face *who* I was. I could consider this journey anywhere, but I knew I needed to focus to do so. The all-encompassing hours and distractions of my career would leave little time for soul-searching. I also realized that my career had been based on motives and desires that I no longer found important. Those things were not going to be my focus; that I knew. God was calling me to change everything. To turn my life upside down and inside out. He was calling me to be a new person. I was utterly frightened and exhilarated by the thought of this new journey.

I knew what I had to do, so I turned, took a deep breath, and walked back to the house. When I went inside, I asked God to help me with the words for this extremely important phone call, and then I dialed the number for my business partner. When he answered the phone, I told him of my decision to remain on the farm.

He sighed. "I knew this was the decision you would make."

"How did you know when I didn't make the decision until just now?"

"If you were coming back, you would've been here by now. I heard a change in your voice after your grandmother died. I don't know how to describe it, but I did."

Very quietly, but with absolute assurance, I said, "I *have* changed."

"Yes, you have. And I think it's good. I hear peace in your voice, Lydia. If staying on that farm is what you want, then I'm happy for you. I truly am. But we do need to decide how we are going to proceed."

"Why don't you ask—" I cut myself off, realizing this shouldn't be my decision. "Why don't you think about someone you trust and can work with? If that person works out temporarily, then you can ask him or her to be your new partner. We can work out the financial details later."

"But what if you decide to come back later?"

"We'll figure it out then. In the meantime, you need a business partner, and it's not me."

"Thank you, Lydia. Thank you for thinking of me and the business. It's been a challenge running this place by myself. Look, I need to go, but I want you to know that I wish you the best, and I'm guessing some amazing things are going to happen to you out there on that farm. Will you stay in touch?"

"I will. I might not be there with you, but I'll still be curious about how it's going."

And with that, two long-time partners said goodbye, and I was officially on a new journey.

I sat without moving for several minutes after I hung up the phone. Aunt Lu walked in the room and saw me just sitting there with a faraway look on my face.

"Is everything all right, dear?" she asked.

"Excuse me?" I said, looking up at her. "Oh, yes, I'm fine. I just told my business partner that I'm not coming back. I hope it's all right with you that I continue to stay here."

Aunt Lu smiled. "Oh, my dear, it is more than all right. I'm delighted that you're staying—just delighted. Actually, thrilled is the word." She rushed over and squeezed me with all her might.

"Oh my," I gasped. "I don't think I've ever had a hug like that!"

"I'm just so happy that I can't help myself," she said.

I smiled and said, "I'm glad you approve. I'm pleased that the decision is made, but I need some fresh air. I think I'll head back outside."

"Life always looks better when you get some fresh air inside you. And Lydia . . ."

"Yes?"

"I'm truly very happy that you are staying."

"Me too, Aunt Lu. Me too."

I returned to the orchard and sat against the largest tree I could find. It was so easy to pray while sitting under these beautiful apple trees. I suddenly wondered why I had always been drawn to this orchard. Why did I find it so easy to pray here? Being outside without distractions made it easier to pray. It was certainly easier to hear God without the noise of our modern world. Sitting here, under my beloved trees, made it so easy to see the beauty of God's work. I could see the amazing colors of all the flowers from the orchard. I could feel the strength of the trees. I could sense the immense size of the wonderful creation He had made and the nearness of God and His love for me. Peace. God's amazing peace was as near as my breath when I sat among these trees.

I felt led to pray out loud. "Thank you, God, for guiding me in my decision to stay. Now, where would you have me go from here?"

I had a strange sense of knowing. It was as if God Himself told me to tend to my farm, my gardens, and my soul, and the next step would be given to me soon. It was exhilarating. There really was a purpose for staying here. *Well, of course there is,* I told myself.

Once again, I felt excited and scared at the same time. I had followed only my own plan for so long. I wondered when this next step would be revealed, but I decided not to dwell on that. What I needed to do was simply make sure my eyes and ears and heart were always ready to see, hear, and feel what God had to say. And I reminded myself that I needed to think more about being than doing and exactly what that meant. Since my years of running were behind me, I really needed to discover who I was. That discovery might take some time.

At that moment, Sam pulled in the driveway and drove back to the barn. He could see the orchard from that part of the drive, so I gave him a wave, inviting him to join me. He climbed out of his truck and walked over to me.

"Isn't this orchard and those flowerbeds over there just gorgeous?" I asked.

"Don't tell me you're just now realizing this," Sam said with a grin.

"Well, not really. But in a way, I'm seeing them differently."

"Let me give you a hand up, and we can have some coffee." He reached down to help me up from the dirt.

"Do I look like I need a cup of coffee?" I asked, brushing my hands off on my jeans.

"No, but I need some, and I'd like your company," Sam told me.

"In that case, I think I do need another cup."

As we walked toward the house, I said, "Sam, I want to tell you something."

He stopped and waited for my next sentence.

"I called my business partner this morning and told him I wasn't returning."

Sam appeared pleased with my announcement, but when he spoke, he simply said, "Good for you. I hope you'll be happy living here."

I didn't know what was going through his mind, but it seemed like he'd wanted to say more. I wanted to say more too, but I remembered Gail's advice about waiting to pursue a relationship until other parts of my life were settled. I knew that was good advice.

"Let's go see if Aunt Lu has been doing her usual baking," I suggested.

Sure enough, Aunt Lu had been baking enough to nearly fill the kitchen. I quickly spotted one of my favorite breads—lemon poppy seed.

"Did you bake this bread for someone special, or could Sam and I have some?" I called to my aunt, who was in another room.

Aunt Lu yelled back, "I can't think of anyone more special than the two of you. You can have as much as you'd like."

I grinned. "I could eat this whole loaf."

"You better save some for me," he said.

"I'd be ill if I ate this whole thing," I said, pulling two plates from the cabinet.

I set the plates and two forks on the table and then looked over at Sam. "So, what's new with you today?"

"I just hadn't checked in with you in a while, and I wanted to see if everything was going well around here."

"Everything is great. Now that I've decided to stay, it's as if a huge burden has been lifted. I've been so torn with feeling like I should leave and get back to my business but also feeling drawn to stay here. I debated it for so long. Now, it's as if I'm seeing this place for the first time."

Sam's expression grew serious. "Well, now that you're seeing it for the first time, do you see things that need to be changed?"

"No. I'm just enjoying the view."

Sam nodded and smiled. "You look more . . . rested, I guess. Maybe it's just that the weight of the decision is off your shoulders."

We enjoyed our bread and coffee and talked about the crops and other things. Then Sam looked at me from across the table and studied my face for a moment. He seemed to be weighing something over in his mind. But just as I opened my mouth to ask him about it, he set his coffee cup on the table and scooted his chair back rather abruptly.

"Well, I've loafed long enough. I need to go," he said, his eyes not quite meeting my gaze. "If you see something that you don't like the looks of, just let me know."

I didn't get up to see him out. For some reason, I found myself glued to the chair and simply watched him leave. I realized that I enjoyed Sam's company. *He's a nice person to share a cup of coffee with*, I thought.

Although I replayed our conversation a few more times, still wondering why he'd left so quickly, I was finally able to put it out of my mind and work on other things. I decided to confer with Aunt Lu about what needed to be done around the old farmstead. Many repairs, such as a new roof, had been postponed during Grandmother's illness, and I felt that things needed to be addressed before real problems arose. Together, we discussed the issues and who might help with the necessary improvements. We both felt a sense of accomplishment that we were lovingly taking care of our home.

As we made notes about repairs, Aunt Lu suddenly asked, "Would you like to invite Sam to dinner?"

I was surprised by the question and nearly dropped my pen on the table. "Did you and Grandmother often have him over for dinner?"

"Well, not in a long time. I just thought you might like to invite him."

"Are you trying to suggest something?" I asked. I hoped she couldn't tell how much I wanted to invite him.

"As far as I can tell, you haven't had dinner with a nice man in a long time."

"Aunt Lu, I'm not sure I've ever had dinner with a nice man."

"That's exactly what I'm talking about! And that Sam *is* a nice man."

"Yes, he is. Look, I need to work out some things with myself first. Then I'll think about it."

"That's fine. I understand. Just don't wait too long. You're not getting any younger, you know." Aunt Lu grinned.

If she hadn't said that with a wink and a grin on her face, I might have been upset. As it was, it was difficult to be angry with my aunt.

Chapter 28

THE NEXT MONTH FOUND ME working on the farm. I noted some other repairs that would eventually be needed, and I also found myself thinking about extending the flowerbeds and wondering what flowers I might choose.

I also spent a good amount of time reading the Bible and praying. As a few days turned into weeks, I knew I was right where I needed to be. I could feel myself healing, and my past aches lessening with each day. Although I had no idea why yet, I had a strong feeling that God was preparing me for something. I decided not to worry about what it could be because God had been faithful in giving me answers and assurances about my path, and I knew the information I needed would come at the right time.

I needed faith to keep walking my new path, and I received strong affirmations from my community and church family. People would often tell me how glad they were that I had decided to stay. Many people also commented on how happy I looked. To themselves, I would sometimes hear them say they had *never* seen me look so happy and at peace.

In addition to praying, I also decided to follow Mr. Carroll's advice to start writing. How to begin chronicling my journey eluded me a bit, so I decided simply to journal everything that I had thought about and learned since I had been home. Mr.

Carroll was right: it truly was a cathartic experience. Journaling also made me realize how much I enjoyed the writing process. Mr. Carroll was correct about that as well.

I spent as much time sitting in Grandmother's rocking chair as I could. Gazing out the window of her room, I felt her wisdom and presence there with me, and that brought me even more peace. At times, I would feel guilt over missed opportunities of spending time with her. But each time those feelings set in, I would remind myself that God's timing was perfect. I had come home in time to see her, and I had been in a perfect place to truly hear her message to me. I knew that my grandmother was somehow aware of my transformation and was thrilled by it.

I continued to learn from her through the journal lessons she'd left for me. The entry simply titled "Being" was especially enjoyable and enlightening.

There is so much emphasis on doing *in our current culture. Shoe commercials tell us to "do." People ask us, "What do you do?" Careers are built and ruined on how much or how little you do. From my perspective, you, my dear Lydia, have lived your life doing. How much can you accomplish? Who can you impress with your achievements? Yes, I know, career paths are built on this. I would like you to stop and reflect on being for a minute. What does it mean simply to be?*

I believe it means that you are completely aware of the moment and are 100 percent present in it. Your senses are alive! You are observing, listening, examining, feeling, and fully aware of every aspect of the moment. You are active and responding to what is going on around you.

Most of us live at a superficial level. We see life only on the surface, and then we act on what we see. That is simply doing.

Being is not necessarily the act of doing nothing. It is all about being incredibly present in the moment. It means giving the soul eyes and ears so that you can fully process the deeper meaning of a moment. Being requires living at a deeper, more reflective, more authentic soul level.

Being is not simply living through a moment. It is being so in tune and present that you are aware of God everywhere and that you are fully aware of what God is calling forth from you in that moment or situation. Being is seeing God in each person, in all of nature, and in the mundane everyday lives we live. I challenge you to reflect on this. I believe that God asks us to live in a being state more than a doing state. When we are present in the moment, we are much more likely to hear God's will and lessons for us.

Another aspect of being involves who God calls us to be. Again, I am not talking about a job. I'm referring to the type of people we are meant to be. What type of spirits or blessings did God give us to share with others? Who God call us to be could perhaps manifest itself in many ways. This may take time to decipher, but I believe it is important work.

Dear Lydia, I'm going to propose something that may make you angry, but again I ask you to think about it to see if you find any wisdom in this. I think you should walk away from your career for a time. If you continue *that routine, you will simply continue that routine. You will have no time or energy to be if you continue as you have been. Here, on this farm, you will have time and energy to slow down and to reflect. You will be able to think deeper than you would otherwise. I'm not asking you to do this forever, just for a time.*

Be, Lydia. Be in the moment. Don't worry about doing. You have accomplished more than anyone else I know. Now, it is time to be.

With love, my dear one,
Grandmother

My first response when I had finished reading was that I'd already spent a little time thinking about being instead of doing. Though I hadn't yet fully flushed out such a deep meaning as Grandmother had, I'd already sensed the significance of this topic. I thought I understood what she was saying to me, and I agreed with her. It was more important to *be* than to *do*. Who God designed me to be is much more important than any career could ever be. I thought about that for a while. It was a shocking revelation for a woman whose entire life was built around her career. That was simply more evidence that God was helping me turn my life upside down.

I smiled when I thought of Grandmother's suggestion to stay on the farm so that I could slow down and reflect. "I'm well ahead of you on that subject, Grandmother," I said aloud. My only question was, how should I move forward with this lesson?

Chapter 29

SINCE I HAD DECIDED TO STAY on the farm, I asked one of my former business associates to clean out my apartment. It was a relatively easy task because I had never really turned my apartment into a home. I owned few possessions. The arrangement was to have my clothes shipped to the farm, but everything else was to be donated to charity. I had no need for more furniture; and honestly, I was looking for a new life, and those few possessions were a tie to the past.

When my clothes arrived, I realized all I really had was my work wardrobe. There were few clothes to wear for the more casual life I was living, so I called Gail to see if she would like to go shopping. The nearest serious shopping center was a forty-five-minute drive away, and I thought it would be nice to have company for the trip. I decided this would be a good time to discuss the "Being" lesson with my friend. I wanted assistance with processing the information.

"Any interest in hearing about another of Grandmother's lessons?" I asked as we drove.

"You know I'd love to hear it!"

"Well, this one was titled 'Being.' Grandmother talked about being in the moment and living a deeper, more reflective life. She used words and phrases such as *observing, listening, noticing*

God in everything, and *being aware of what God is calling forth from you in the moment.* I think I have an idea of what she was talking about. The other day, I saw all the flowers on the farm in a new way, and I felt like I was seeing them for the first time. It was as if I saw them in 3D, while everything else around them was two-dimensional. In fact, everything else sort of blurred into the background. I was struck by how they looked and how they seemed to pop out to grab my attention. Their beauty caused me to stop and think about God's presence in nature."

"That's an awesome description. Go on," Gail prompted.

"Being able to see a flower and experience its beauty at a deeper level is one thing, but how do you process the meaning of this lesson? Grandmother also talked about being the type of person God called me to be. Not necessarily as in a job, but rather, more like the essence of who I was designed to be. She mentioned having a blessing that I am supposed to share. Do you think she's talking about a calling or something? I'm struggling to wrap my brain around it."

Gail nodded. "I think you're right to spend time thinking about this. It's not as simple as it seems."

"You can say that again!" I said.

"It's not as simple as it seems." She giggled. I glanced at her, and we both laughed.

"I'm sorry, Lydia. I've spent too much time with teenagers and their quirky sense of humor."

"No apologies needed. The conversation was getting too serious."

"No, not at all. It's a great subject, but I also may need to think about it. I've just started doing some reading on using to the fullest the gifts God gave us. God has given us all a blessing, or in other words, a gift. There might be different ways we could use our blessings, but they all relate to the paths and purposes God has for us. Perhaps what your grandmother was trying to say was that the blessing is the *being* part. We need to spend our time and energy and prayer discovering those blessings or gifts. How we use them isn't as important as discovering and using them in some way."

I pulled into a parking spot at the shopping center, turned to Gail, and said, "Thanks for the advice. It's as clear as a mud puddle."

This time, it was Gail's turn to have a good chuckle.

We had a full, successful day of shopping and snacking on unhealthy mall foods and then headed home. While we shopped, we shared more than time together. We also shared stories and laughter.

On the ride home, Gail decided to share some thoughts on a more serious topic.

"Lydia, there's something that I've been thinking about lately. After spending the day together, I see the absolute importance of it. We need community."

"I'm afraid I've rubbed off on you," I said. "After today, you should be thinking about fashion rules or something. This 'community' concept sounds pretty deep."

"I'm serious."

"I believe you. Maybe too serious."

"Let me bounce this off of you," Gail said. "I think people are a type of herd animal. We need to share ideas with each other, just like you and I do. We need others to help us learn and to hold us accountable. And you know what else?"

"What?"

"In the reading I've been doing, the author believes that, as a community, we each reflect a part of God. God is so big that we each cannot be a complete representation of Him alone. But the gifts and blessings that He has given each of us allows us to reflect that part of Him. So, as a community, we reflect God as a whole. By ourselves, we are only a fragment. We need a community to be whole."

It was good that I was at a stop sign with no one behind me because I just sat and stared at Gail. I realized there was something big in what she had said, but I didn't quite grasp what it meant. There seemed to be real wisdom in this concept of community and being able to reflect God as a whole, but how would it work?

"Gail, what would we need to do? How would this 'community' work?"

"I don't think the details of the community matter as much as the idea that we need a community of believers to be complete. Through a community, we can see and experience God. Since God is so big, no one person can reflect God to us. We need an entire community to do that. Again, alone we are only a fragment, and that's not enough. We need a community."

I sat there thinking about this idea. Perhaps this was yet another reason why it was so painful to simply run away from everything and everyone I knew, including myself. Perhaps this would help explain why it was so incredibly painful to isolate myself; what I truly needed and craved to feel complete was a community. Grandmother had often shared her belief in the importance of community, and she encouraged me to be a part of one. I never really understood the importance of it until now. As for words, I had none. I finally realized I was still stopped at the stop sign. I pulled forward and simply replied, "I'm speechless. I don't know what else to say."

Gail smiled. "I guess I can cross 'leaving a lawyer speechless' off my bucket list."

Chapter 30

AUNT LU AND I WERE BOTH EXHAUSTED from the hours we'd spent canning and freezing the bounty from our large garden, and we welcomed the rainy weather we were experiencing because it meant we could take a break from the pace we had been working. Right now, it was simply too muddy to be in the garden. I took the opportunity to sit in Grandmother's rocking chair and gaze out her window once again.

I remembered another rainy day not so long ago when Sam had told me, "Just because it's raining doesn't mean it rains every day." What a great analogy for life! Just because there was a bad day or there were bad times didn't mean that every day was bad.

I sipped my coffee and smiled, acknowledging the woman I was becoming—my true self as God designed me to be. My past was in the past. Through God's grace, I had found redemption from it, and I was finally free to embrace my future and move forward. Although I had been the victim of rape, I didn't have to live as a victim. That night was not my fault. It is tragic that so many women blame themselves for being victims of rape and abuse. I had done so for years, but I had finally realized a mighty truth—it was not my fault.

What about all those other times? some voice deep inside me asked. *Those other times weren't rape.*

I acknowledged that all those other times were mistakes. In fact, they were huge mistakes, and I had made many of them. Though I hadn't realized it at the time, I had been seeking love, affirmation, and someone to trust. I had been searching for something I didn't even realize I needed. I kept looking for what I needed to feel whole, but my biggest mistake was that I was looking for the wrong thing in the wrong places. Should I be damned forever for the mistakes I'd made?

Absolutely not. People make mistakes, but as Grandmother had said, there is no action or moment that is beyond God's desire and capacity for redemption. His redemptive love is for everyone! With it, we can rise above our worst moments.

The shame and guilt I'd felt so deeply for so long had caused me to become stuck in a cycle of poor choices. Now, I was finally able to move forward. It was time to let God's love and grace wash over me. It had just taken time for this strong-willed and independent woman to fully digest the reality of God's grace and love. It was exactly what I'd needed to overcome the shame and guilt I had lived with for so many years. I knew God had forgiven me, and I was working at forgiving myself. It would take time to process my emotions and restore my broken values. I realized now that I kept repeating the past because I had never repaired my values, especially my value of trust. Yes, I had been stuck, but I was moving on now with God's grace.

As I rocked in the chair, I remembered the author presentation I had attended with my friend while we were in high school. The longer I thought about it, the more I realized the parallels between the presenter and myself were remarkable. We were both raised by our grandparents because our parents were not able to raise us.

We both had been raped. Yes, we'd both faced some horrendous times.

Many years ago, I had heard Joan, the speaker, say that she'd chosen to view what happened to her as a stepping-stone that she could stand on to become closer to God. I smiled, realizing that, although it had taken me years, I had finally transformed my situation from a stumbling block into a stepping-stone as well. Some lessons took time to learn.

Tears welled in my eyes yet again as I reflected on my past. My inner child sobbed over what had been taken from me and for the pain I'd endured. Redemption didn't completely erase the pain, but it made it survivable. The pain was a part of me, I knew, but only a part. There was life above and beyond it. I would no longer allow it to define me. It was time for me to move forward and focus on discovering God's purpose for me. His grace and love had lifted me above the chaos of my past.

I had faced some very scary things in my life. Perhaps I hadn't tried some dangerous physical activities, but in a way, facing my internal demons was much more frightening. I stood up to them and fought them. *God and I are a good team. We can handle scary*, I thought. I closed my eyes and thanked God for all His gifts. Although I would never regain the innocence I lost on that night all those years ago, God was indeed mending my shattered soul, and His unconditional love was shining brightly through the cracks He was healing. Those cracks represented a painful past, but I was whole and complete.

Chapter 31

THE LETTER ARRIVED IN THE MAIL on the first Tuesday in September. It looked official. The nearby city of Richland wanted to dig a well just down the road from my farm. Their intent was to tap into the underground aquifer and pipe the water thirty miles back to the city. I was outraged. There was a hearing in two weeks and I had little time to prepare a fight, but I fully intended to go to war. Although I would conduct research to confirm my fears, I was certain that this would drain the well on my farm and probably the wells of many of my neighbors. "You can't fight city hall" wasn't a phrase in my vocabulary. I would fight with everything I could, and I was determined to win.

My first step in building my case was to call the leading scientific university in the state. I spoke to several professors and took pages of notes from these discussions. The professors recommended several websites, and I spent hours searching for relevant information. I needed to prepare a great deal of research to fight against the city's experts, and I knew I would have to hire my own experts as well.

I also called many of my neighbors and explained to them what the letter meant. My information and determination to beat this proposal brought them comfort. They all felt that tapping into the aquifer was an invasion and that the city looked down on them. They were sure the city thought this would be an easy victory. Everyone I called told me they were counting on me and that they would back me any way they could.

I spent probably eighteen hours a day working on my arguments. There was little time for anything except a few hours of sleep, and I even ate at the computer. When Sam stopped by to see how I was doing, I asked Aunt Lu to explain that I couldn't stop working. The deadline was looming, and I had so much to learn. The only phone calls I would take were about the case.

When the day of the hearing finally arrived, I entered the room, approached the hearing officer, and informed him that I was representing the landowners. The city's lead attorney flashed me a condescending smirk. I knew what that meant: "Oh, how sweet; they brought their little lawyer with them." What they didn't know was that I hadn't come to the hearing alone. I was armed with two leading underground aquifer experts in the state, as well as several members of the farm community.

Finally, the time came for me to present my motions and evidence, and when I did, the city's lawyers stopped smiling. They glanced at each other with expressions that said this wasn't going to be the simple formality they had expected.

What was originally scheduled for a one-day hearing was continued and then drew on day after day. With tenacity, I cross-examined each expert the city presented. The witnesses I presented for the landowners were considered among the best in their fields, and their evidence and testimonies could not be swayed.

At the beginning of the fifth day of hearings, with the prospect of me bringing in even more experts, the city withdrew its request. The lawyers announced that the city had decided to consider other options. I thought the edges of the hearing officer's mouth gave the slightest hint of a smile.

"Request for dismissal granted," the hearing officer said.

The fight was over with that simple statement, and I smiled for the first time in days. I turned to greet the small group of farmers who had come that day. Since the hearing had continued for so long, they'd had to take turns attending.

As I walked toward the small group, one of the city's lawyers approached me. He told me that his firm was always looking for tenacious attorneys like me to join them.

"Would you like to have lunch so we could discuss the details of our offer?" he asked.

"I'm flattered," I said. "But let me think about it. Right now, I need to talk to my clients."

"Of course. Here's my card. Please call me soon. We have several pending cases that we could assign to you."

"Thank you. I will call you."

I then joined my clients, and they all congratulated me on a job well done. I could not remember a work victory that had brought me such joy.

In the car, I finally had time to reflect on the past few days. This was the first time in my career I had fought for "ordinary" people. These were not the super-rich, special-interest groups that I had often worked for in the past. They weren't international businesses with millions of dollars in profits at stake. These were ordinary, hard-working people who were fighting for the continuation of their ways of life. They were fighting for the right to something so simple but crucial for their survival—water.

I realized, for the first time in my career, that I genuinely believed in my cause. These friends and neighbors had needed my expertise, knowledge, and tenacity. They had given me a true sense of purpose. They had needed me, not for some greedy purpose, but simply to maintain their modest livelihoods and homes. I had previously worked with rather impersonal clients, most of whom I barely knew. These, however, were my neighbors. I worshipped with them. I had fellowship with them. They were my friends.

How many other times could my neighbors use my help? There would not be many situations like this one, but what about the little things? Would they take comfort in having a friend write their wills, knowing that I had their best interests in mind? I felt the now-familiar prick of heat behind my eyes and wiped away a tear. This acknowledgment that I cared deeply for my neighbors was powerful.

I suddenly had a sense of knowing about my God-given blessing. God had placed me here to bring comfort to others. Although I had been thinking I was being called to a new profession, I realized I could use my training to bring comfort to these people, my people. My friends and neighbors. I had been wondering about the next steps for months, and here they were. I could use my skills and gifts right here. *A purpose, right here.* I felt a deep sense of peace and joy, and I smiled.

As soon as I arrived back at the house, I pulled out the business card I'd been handed and called the office. I explained who I was to the receptionist and asked to leave a message. It was simple: "Thank you for your kind offer, but I'm not seeking a position at this time."

With that task completed, I told Aunt Lu that I needed some fresh air. There had been no time to be outside since the letter from the city had arrived. I missed spending time in the orchard, and I missed gazing at God's amazing nature. Yes, I *could* have a business here that would still allow me time to enjoy nature. It would be possible to have a small private practice and still have time for the things I was just learning to enjoy. I could do both!

Realizing that I could feel so truly blessed by using my talents to help someone was a new, powerful thought. All these years, I had used my training and skills for distorted and unhealthy purposes. I had pursued power and greed instead of lifting others up. To avoid feeling like a victim, I had fought to gain power so that I could be in control. I told myself that I worked hard because I had to provide for myself. In reality, I worked hard because it gave me the illusion that I was in control and that I was the only person I needed to trust. Being a workaholic was how I had survived my pain and brokenness. It was how I had coped with my broken core values.

Now, perhaps for the first time, I felt needed by others and realized how incredibly happy that made me feel. My needs to receive and give comfort were aligned with my gifts and training. God had shown me that my gifts and skills could be used for His purpose and not simply for my own. For the first time, I felt the true joy of having my core values align with God's true purpose for me.

I also realized that I completely trusted God. I believed and trusted that God wanted the best for me and would guide me toward what was best. I smiled when I realized this meant turning over control to Him. Thinking I was in control was simply an illusion anyway. Though I knew there would be times when I would be afraid, I still trusted Him.

Something else occurred to me as I reflected: this farm was a metaphor for my life. I had run away from this place and from my past, both literally and figuratively. I had moved away and turned my back on it all, trying to escape my suffocating pain. Since I had stopped running, I had found peace here—in God's nature, in my family and church community, in becoming who I was meant to be, and in God's embrace. This farm that I thought represented my past and that I wanted to escape had become a part of my healing and my future. I had come home—to this farm, to my true self, and to God.

Chapter 32

IT WAS A GLORIOUS FALL DAY. The trees were showing their beautiful red, gold, and orange colors. It seemed that even the trees themselves were praising God for this wonderful weather. The farmers were almost done with harvest. Our community had been through a battle over water rights, and we had been victorious. Everyone was still in a spirit of praise.

Reverend Peters had asked me to sing at church. In fact, he had begged me for weeks. I finally agreed because I had felt so many blessings. I had wholeheartedly accepted God's love, and I was so blessed to leave my shame and fear behind. The song I shared reflected my feelings.

After the sermon, I stood to sing. I prayed that those attending would be moved by the song.

Shame had been my constant shadow
For years pain made me less than whole.
My past had haunted and tortured
No peace could be found in my soul.

When my burden was too much to carry,
God came to comfort me.
He whispered a love song to my soul
And told my pain to flee.

I was freed from the
Depths of my shame.
I was freed from the
Fears that bound.
I was freed from the
Worries of unknown tomorrow.
I was freed because I am God's own.

Several church members nodded and smiled. They may not have heard this song before, but they certainly understood it. The worries of tomorrow and the pain from the past could most definitely lead a person to feel no peace in his or her soul.

Life still isn't easy
But it's lighter since that day
When God helped me lay down my burdens
And I chose to follow His way.

When the skies are cloudy
When confusion and trouble come,
My blessings outweigh my hardships
Because God is my steadfast home.

I am free from the
Depths of my shame.
I am free from the
Fears that bound.
I am free from the
Worries of unknown tomorrow.
I am free because I am God's own.

Many of the older ladies reached into their purses for their handkerchiefs. Aunt Lu had a huge smile on her face. She knew more than anyone the healing I was experiencing. I hoped the others in the church had also noticed my transformation since I had been home.

With tears in his eyes, Reverend Peters stood and went to the pulpit. This song seemed to have touched him.

"Friends, I think our friend has preached her own sermon here today. Even a pastor occasionally needs to be reminded that he is free from the worries of tomorrow and from the burdens of the past.

"Not only was that a magnificent song, but I think we can all recognize that Lydia is living those words. Now, I feel called to ask anyone who wants to celebrate God's love or to recommit themselves to following His path to come and pray with me at the communion rail."

I was the first to rise. I had already decided to follow the path God had designed for me, but I felt drawn to take this "official" step. And though the decision was a personal one, I wanted to take this physical and visual step as I was surrounded by my faith community. Several others also came forward.

Reverend Peters knelt with us, and while he was praying, I felt the presence of the Holy Spirit. Suddenly, I had a vision of the Samaritan woman at the well. In my mind, I watched as she questioned Jesus about why he had asked her, a woman of Samaria, to give him, a Jew, a drink. I saw Jesus acknowledge her many mistakes involving men. He gave her forgiveness and filled her with living water. The burdens of her sins were lifted, and she would never thirst again.

I wept silently as I felt God's embrace. I realized that I was like the woman at the well. My many mistakes had filled me with shame. While the Samaritan woman went to draw water at noon when no one else would be at the well, I had built emotional walls around myself to hide from others. Yes, I had much in common with the Samaritan woman. Just like her, I was more than forgiven. I was also filled with living water. I was experiencing my own resurrection—a gift of new life as I accepted that I was a child of God and that He loved me unconditionally. A no-matter-what love. Being a victim of a crime and a victim of myself no longer mattered. It didn't matter that I had created so much of the chaos in my life. I was a child of God—loved and embraced! My despair, pain, and shame had been replaced with hope, peace, and joy.

I knew that life would not suddenly become a fairy tale. There would still be hardships and pain, and it would not always be an easy path. But I also knew the hardships would be easier to manage because I was no longer as focused on the worries of the world. I was focused on what it meant to be loved by God. The peace I felt in my soul was difficult to describe, but it was powerful and something to celebrate.

My priorities had changed. My soul had been transformed. I knew my life would be different because I was walking through this life with God, and I was loved.

And I knew with certainty—it was well with my soul.

LETA BUHRMANN

letawrites.com
facebook.com/LetaBWrites

CPSIA information can be obtained
at www.ICGtesting.com
Printed in the USA
BVHW031207020622
638743BV00014B/157

9 781955 648004